The Liberation
of Little Heaven

The Liberation
of Little Heaven

and other stories

Mark Jacobs

The following stories have been previously published, some of them in a slightly different form:
"The Liberation of Little Heaven" in *The American Literary Review* (Volume 9, Number 2, Fall 1998); "Two Dead Indians" in *Kiosk* (Volume 11, 1998.); "Mengele Dies Again" in *The American Literary Review* (Volume 7, Number 2, Fall 1996); "The Rape of Reason" in *North Dakota Quarterly* (Volume 63, Number 2, Spring 1996); "Down in Paraguay" in *Buffalo Spree Magazine* (Volume 27, Number 3, Fall 1993); "Dove of the Back Streets" in *The Kenyon Review* (Vol. XX, No. 3/4, Summer/ Fall 1998); "The Ballad of Tony Nail" in *Crucible* (Volume 33, Fall 1997); "Solidarity in Green" in *The Southern Review* (Volume 32, Number 1, Winter 1996); "How Birds Communicate" in *The Iowa Review* (Volume 27, Number 3, 1997) and "Looking for Lourdes" in *The American Literary Review* (Volume VIII, Number 2, Fall 1997).

Published by
Soho Press
853 Broadway
New York, NY 10003

Library of Congress Cataloging-in-Publication Data
Jacobs, Mark, 1951–
The liberation of little heaven and other stories / Mark Jacobs.
p. cm.
ISBN 1-56947-135-5 (alk. paper)
1. Bolivia—Social life and customs—Fiction.   2. Paraguay—Social life and customs—Fiction.   3. Honduras—Social life and customs—Fiction.   I. Title.
PS3560.A2549L52   1999
813'.54—dc21   98-39432
CIP

For Thomas, Elisa, and Matthew
Eyes to see, a tongue to say, and all the heart

Contents

the liberation of
little heaven

The timing was what
made her marvel. On the near edge of the moment in which Aramí
Bedoya was sure she was going to snap, a messenger arrived. She
was used to things being hard, and her hopes were like her expectations, small enough to fit inside a powdered-milk can. But the pressure of Don Andrés in the park like a statute of ugly was more than
she could bear. There was too much remembering, too little forgetting. Then here came a messenger.

It was the siesta hour. Heat rose in crinkled waves from the
Paraguay River and dissipated in the December sky, which was
harsh and unrelievedly blue. Under just such a sky, she presumed,
was baby Jesus born. The first time they carried him out of the sta-
ble and he looked up, the light would have scalded his eyes, God
the Father thereby reminding him what he was in for by agreeing to
come down to save such a world. She was not a religious woman,

not in the rosary-and-reverence sense of the word, which made the visit of the messenger that much harder to figure.

Maria de la Paz and Maria Carmen were already asleep on the apple crates she had converted into beds. They lay sprawled on their backs like cats, hip to hip, sweating. The flat tin roof of the shack collected heat, drawing it down inside to cook them slowly. Any day now we'll wake up well done, Aramí thought. For a moment she watched the same pulse beat in the thin blue veins in their upturned wrists. She didn't have the heart to wake them to send them after their younger sister, Maria Mercedes, who was born a wanderer, the kind of child guaranteed to bring down worry on a mother's head.

Aramí looked for her sandals, didn't find them. This is what democracy brings, she told herself, meaning the terror. She intended no irony or bitterness; it was only an observation.

She left the two older girls to sleep and reluctantly climbed the dirt path out of La Chacarita, the *barrio* along the river where poor people like herself lived a hunkering kind of city life. Over the stone fence she crossed into Parque Caballero, which also napped in the heat. The grass under the big eucalyptus trees was parched brown, the gravel baked, the iron arms of the park benches were hot enough to burn a person's flesh.

Anybody who had a place to be was elsewhere. One lone drunk with bare feet like stumpy tubers slept on the ground in a patch of shade with a straw sombrero covering his face to keep out the light, both hands cradling an empty bottle of cane whiskey as if to dream back the relief he felt when he drank it. No Maria Mercedes. Aramí scuffed across the dry grass, which complained in a low voice she heard distinctly since at the moment there was no traffic noise. No Maria Mercedes. How far could a five-year-old wander?

And then he was there. She thought she had herself under control, that she could withstand the sight of him. She could not. This was what democracy brought her, she insisted to herself as if it made sense, the terror.

He chose a different bench to rest on every time he came to the park, the kind of thing a person with a spotted conscience would do. The thought made her wonder whether he had a conscience at all. Maybe there were things a person could do that killed the conscience, and the shell of a human being that survived never felt the lack. If that was possible . . . He did not see her. She stood behind a tree and studied him. For the moment she was able to breathe.

He was old, decrepit old, old in a way that made her think of garbage rotting the way it rotted in La Chacarita because there was no place to take it. His liver-spotted hands shook, his white hair had a yellow cast and needed cutting. He walked with a cane these days. It rested on his knees. For a moment she imagined that its knobby head was a hollow-eyed skull, but it was only a gnarled wood bulb. Unless it was a skull. His skin, she observed, was thick and ugly like the skin of an animal that needed protection from a hostile environment. It hung in sagging folds on his body, on his arms, below his chin. Saint Ugly, she named him at that moment; San Feo, meaning evil. She was still breathing normally.

Then Maria Mercedes was there. She had picked up a long, crooked stick, into which she stuck a green beer bottle. The girl was proud of her invention, waving her glass flag in the air to catch someone's attention, but the only one there to notice was Don Andrés. She shuffled in his direction head cocked sideways, proud and eager. Aramí stepped out from behind the eucalyptus and stopped breathing.

Actually what happened was the air she sucked in wouldn't go down her throat into her lungs. It stayed in her mouth, gagging her, while she became quickly dizzy, then faint, and she thought she was going to fall over. Automatically her hand cupped to cover the bad spot on her face. Both Don Andrés and Maria Mercedes were watching her. The girl had stopped walking. You don't know me, she wanted to scream at him, which was crazy. But the words couldn't get past the air clogging her mouth, making her tongue heavy. If Maria Mercedes took one more step in his direction she was going to snap.

The messenger was a kind of miracle, if a person believed in miracles. Aramí did not. She was a woman, out of nowhere there in the park next to Aramí. She was beautiful: tall and slim and straight, her black hair so long down her back it might never have been cut, in a plain white dress the hem of which brushed the grass. Her feet were bare. Her skin was the palest brown, her black eyes angry and intelligent; Aramí knew from the eyes she could hide nothing from her. She looked, it occurred to Aramí, the way she herself might have looked if she'd had any luck in her life. It had been her looks that caused the problem in the first place.

Aramí felt a wave of envy rising like nausea in her body until she noticed that she was breathing again, almost normally, and that neither her daughter nor Don Andrés could see the woman. That meant she was hers alone, a gift though not a miracle. Mercedes lowered her stick to the ground, and the beer bottle slid off onto the grass. Don Andrés picked up his cane as if to defend himself. In the plane of white sunlight he squinted at Aramí as though she had reminded him of something important, and the woman spoke.

"You could kill him, you know," she told her. To Aramí her voice was like joy, like rejoicing. It was the sound of money clinking in a sack, the deep laugh at the end of an excellent joke, a rooster crowing on a morning when you didn't have to get out of bed. "You're stronger than he is. He's weak now. He's so old his bones are like matchsticks." She rubbed her thumb and index finger together to demonstrate the thinness of Don Andrés's old bones. "You could snap his bones in half if you wanted to, you could do it without even trying. You could kill him."

They both laughed at the notion. That broke the suspension of the moment. Mercedes ran toward her waving her stick, out of striking distance of the decrepit man on the wood-slat bench, who hugged his cane close to his chest now as though he had overheard what the splendid creature told Aramí.

"Mamá," Mercedes whined at her, anxious now that she was found. She tugged on her mother's leg.

Aramí took the time to breathe in, savoring the easy way the air went down her throat and into her lungs. Air was like water, it occurred to her. It had a taste but one you had to stop and think about to appreciate. She appreciated.

★ ★ ★

Too little forgetting because too much remembering. Such as the sand in the road to Asunción from Humaitá in the far corner of Paraguay. The truck in the back of which Aramí rode labored for long stretches over the deep sand, which wanted to trap it. And the deep holes, and the long ruts, as though the road itself didn't want to give her up any more than her mother did. The major told the sergeant to drive slowly. There was no hurry. In San Juan de Ñeembucú they stopped and the major bought her a *gaseosa*. He would have preferred a different assignment. She was perceptive. She saw the revulsion his job caused in him, but it was a foreign thing to her, one more adult strangeness. This was in 1979, before there was democracy.

After all the jolting the warm sweet drink turned her stomach, and she did not forgive the major his kindness. The land through which they were traveling was swampy and wild, and there was a lonesome quality to the little town the exuberant chirping of all the bugs in creation could not disguise. While the driver argued with the owner of the little store that dispensed *gaseosas* Aramí stood next to herself in the road under dappled shade, waiting and watching the thirteen-year-old girl from Humaitá who had been offered the educational opportunity of a lifetime. She felt the lonesomeness of San Juan drip in and fill her up, like a cup. Any month now she was going to have her first period. *Then it will start*, her mother had warned her prophetically, meaning something else than what really happened.

What happened was a visit by the major to her parents. *A good education*, he told them. He did not even convince himself. Her mother shrieked and cried. A better education than anything the girl could get around here. Her father, who worked on someone else's ranch and knew how to cure sick horses better than anybody in the *departamento*, hung his head like a beaten man. Her mother ran out into the patio and screamed the way you did when someone you loved died, which made Aramí aware that she had gained a special status. She understood that the little fillip of pride she felt was wrong, or out of place. The educational opportunity of a lifetime, the major told her beaten father. Aramí watched the tears run down his face, fascinated because she could not remember seeing a man cry. All the way to Asunción she imagined what it would be like if one of the holes were deep enough to swallow the truck, and everything disappeared.

It was a coincidence that the *guarderia* to which the major delivered her was also called Aramí, which meant Little Heaven. A heavy individual with small eyes, calm as a coma, shuffled out to the street to meet her, and she was presented formally to the man everyone called Don Andrés with the same tone of respect that she herself learned quickly to use. She wondered why he was exhausted.

She was relieved to learn she was the youngest girl there. Knowing it made her feel not lucky, exactly, but slightly better armored. There was a school, and a playground, and several slender, passive brown women wearing sandals and pastel sundresses. They were in charge of everything, and their faces betrayed no emotion. What they knew was secret. This was in Lambaré, far from the city center. If you climbed high enough up the enormous mango tree that shaded the playground you could see the Rio Paraguay, a twist of silver the sight of which gave false comfort to Aramí because she knew if she had a boat and went downstream she would come, eventually, to Humaitá.

Everyone knew. They studied with the knowledge of it, played with it, grew up in the shade it cast that was at least as broad and compassing as the shade of the mango but denser and not sheltering. Once before she was taken away a handsome girl with nervous blue eyes and streaks of ashy gold in her dark brown hair tried to make a joke. It wasn't her own, just a thing she borrowed from somebody else, so coming out of her mouth it wasn't funny. He's the father of his country, she laughed into her hand at supper one coolish fall evening. They were drinking cocido tea with their bread and jam, and steam rose from the girl's cup the way Aramí imagined prayers, properly directed, would rise to heaven. *El padre de la patria,* the girl giggled again.

Growing up surrounded by so much beauty, so many exceptional women, had its drawbacks even though Aramí had an objective sense of herself; she could hold her own with any of them. But there was competition, and an unstable hierarchy of beauty and power and privilege, and cruelties inflicted out of jealousy and revenge and ambition and all the other low feelings that could move a person. By temperament preferring to stay on the margin of all that conflict, Aramí understood there was something askew in the head-high attitude of triumph so many of them adopted when a jeep with an officer or two aboard showed up to escort them away.

When she was old enough to make the necessary distinctions she, like the others, learned how to identify those chosen to keep the President himself company. It was always the same flat-faced major who came for them, a man with a concave back and a withered arm who took snuff and sneezed violently coming across the patio. The way it worked, only the best of them, the most perfect and precious, were considered likely to pass the President's discriminating muster. They had to be virgins, of course. Offering him damaged goods was inconceivable. Some of those so chosen went willingly.

Naturally it was not possible for everybody at the *guarderia* to go to the President, hungry as he was. But Don Andrés had other friends, many of them military men but not all. The existence of the school he ran was known around the city. There was no shortage of men looking for what Aramí once heard Don Andrés call comely maidens. Guarderia Aramí was full of comely maidens.

She counted. Seven months after leaving Humaitá Aramí had her first period. Knowing she was vulnerable now, she tried to hide the change from everyone, holding in the feeling of emptying-out loss she would have liked to share with someone old enough to help. But the orphanage had its own *pyragüe*, the informants who assisted the police and the government to keep the Republic free of subversion. (*Pyragüe* was "hairy foot," meaning they did their patriotic duty so quietly a person didn't know they were around.) And there was not enough privacy at the orphanage to conceal much of anything except your thoughts; you had to be careful not to give those away because you'd never get them back. It distressed Aramí that she had no idea who had betrayed her.

Don Andrés called her into his office, in a pleasant brick-and-adobe house out behind the classrooms. "*Nde poraité*," he told her in Guarani.

She tamped down the small satisfaction she felt at being told she was very beautiful. He received her in his red-webbed lawn chair in the back patio, a homely sprawl of banana and orange and grapefruit trees and red flowering santa rita, amid a clutter of white chickens stalked incessantly by a black cock with unusual maroon-colored claws. With each conquest, each rebuff, the cock climbed the dome-topped brick oven and puffed out its chest as if to crow, but no sound ever came, which struck Aramí as proof that something was wrong. The combination of sun and unchecked green growth and hot dusty ground below her feet made her think of home, and if it would not have been dangerous she would have cried. As it was she imagined her tears dropping in the dust, which helped a little.

"I'm going to give you a job," Don Andrés told her, making it sound like a favor for which he ought to be thanked, but she could not bring herself to speak. "Blanca, the one who did the ironing in the house, is no longer here. You will take her place. You will iron for me. There are compensations. The food is better. You can eat whenever you wish to eat."

He took his time about his business, which at the time she did not understand was part of the pleasure for him. He came out to the patio, pulled up his red-ribbed chair, and watched her iron for long stretches of time. He spoke very little. In the evenings he came out to the kitchen, which was also behind the house and as private a place as existed at the orphanage, and asked for something simple: a cup of cocido, a sandwich, an orange peeled. If she was eating he watched her eat. Sometimes he brought things for her, usually something sweet that made her mouth water despite the strength of her resolve to yield nothing.

She yielded, of course. There was no choice. She was a week shy of fourteen. One evening under a pale purple sky in which the stars were coming out one by one, and the laughing and horsing-around sounds of the younger girls playing on the swings was like squeaky music, and an undernourished cat from the neighborhood was rubbing its sides against her legs hoping for a handout, Don Andrés found her in the kitchen. He put one hand gently over her mouth, the other hand on her breast. Both hands squeezed. After a long moment like that he unbuttoned her blouse with what almost felt like tenderness, took off her clothes, then guided her hand to the fat black leather belt around his waist.

Then it will start, she remembered her mother's prophecy. But what started for Aramí on the floor of Don Andrés' kitchen was only a sweaty friction that produced fear and then a terrible loathing that included not just him, not just her, but the wide field of purple sky with its crop of white stars, and the innocent voices of the girls playing a hundred meters away, a hateful sound, and the sweet taste of guayaba jam in the corners of her mouth, and the filthy stuff with which he filled her vagina all the time making cooing noises of pleasure intended to coax her into a state of resignation and complicity. She was almost fourteen, and when he was gone she could not help sobbing. She lay there until it was completely dark. When she got up, she searched in the patio for a rotten mango and bit into it. The huge hunk of putrid fruit she put into her mouth gagged her, and she threw up everything there was to throw up.

The trick was not to remember the things you could not forget.

There were privileges. She was indifferent to them. She existed in a perfect trance that made the familiar routine of work and submission not tolerable but survivable. She learned by listening sideways to the slim brown women who taught the classes that she was unusual. Don Andrés ordinarily tired immediately of the ones he picked for himself, used them up and sent them away, then turned his attention to the next. But he did not tire of Aramí, for which distinction some of the girls envied her. She knew also that that was wrong.

When she was fifteen and still ironing, still eating guayaba jam and waiting to hear him come up behind her with his blind hands, the major who took snuff visited Don Andrés. It was a cool morning, probably August. They sat together inside the house drinking *mate* from a silver straw. She was not asked to serve. After a few minutes of pleasantries both men raised their voices, and the major left in an angry hurry without taking his customary stroll around the grounds, when he liked to look at the orphans. Shopping, the girls called it.

That night it was cold, a fierce wind out of the south that brought in clouds and stirred the dust and killed old people in their sickbeds. Aramí was in the kitchen bundled in a sweater that was too big for her. She was not thinking, because thinking led to feeling, and all the things she had to feel were better cauterized.

"I need a shirt ironed," Don Andrés told her. That surprised her. Often the cold air made him want sex, a form of heat, she assumed, to keep off the weather. And she had pressed his shirts that morning. She heated her iron, and he sat to watch.

"They've told the President about you," he said quietly when she began to work. "He wants to see you."

"I'm not a virgin." Panic came into the kitchen with the cold wind, which dumped it there. She wanted no change. She did not want to meet the President. She did not want anything that would wake her up. Not that she was really asleep.

"It doesn't matter." He shook his head slowly, as though he were already grieving her loss. "You are more beautiful than all the rest, Aramí."

"I'm not," she contradicted him.

"You are, but it's something else you have that works the magic. I don't know what to call it. It's a quality. The President will be taken with you. It cannot be otherwise."

"I won't go," she threatened. She wanted no change.

He sighed, rose from his chair, moved toward her to take the shirt, which she had draped over the edge of the ironing board. But he didn't take it. Instead he enfolded her in his great bulk, familiar to her now as her own body. "I don't want to lose you, Aramí." He reached for the shirt, but what he actually picked up was the hot iron. For a fat man he was quite strong. She was unable to escape his big embrace when he held the iron to her face. He left it there long enough to make a mark that would last forever.

So she didn't meet the President. She didn't know and didn't care what kind of story Don Andrés concocted to explain the accident. He was solicitous nursing the burn on her face. He moved her into a room of her own in his house, and someone else was given her chores. He even had a television set delivered to keep her mind off the pain and the disfigurement. There was something in the man's eyes that had not been there before, something humanly imploring she refused to acknowledge. While she recuperated he did not attempt to have sex with her. She assumed he was saving it up, knew without his needing to say it that the scar on her face would not spoil his attraction to her, that it might make him want her more.

She lived in a bubble of temporary quiescence, and an odd relief flowered inside her.

It took a long time for her face to heal enough that the pain went down. She did not spend much time thinking about how ugly she was going to be, although she avoided mirrors. The first day she got out of bed she was weak, and Don Andrés hovered over her fretting, telling her she mustn't work yet. A new girl in the kitchen brought her something to eat, set it in front of her without a word, and disappeared as if whatever *mal* Aramí had might be catching.

She was stronger by the evening, and the strength gave her thoughts clarity. She thought about her parents, her home, the river in Humaitá, the ranch on which her father worked. She thought about the taste of the rotten mango, and the bestial smell Don Andrés's skin gave off when he was in the throes of sexual excitement, and how she would have liked to hear the stories of the women who taught the classes now that she understood they also were castoffs. All that clear thinking left her alert, so that when the door opened after she was in bed for the night she had a convincing sentence ready that kept him out of her room for one more night.

Little as it was, that success encouraged her. She had no plan, but next day when Don Andrés slept his siesta she went down the street to the little *despensa* to buy a jar of Nescafé for his late afternoon snack. She did not like going to the store; the woman who ran it took too much pleasure in sniffing at her, making plain her disapproval of anyone connected to the orphanage. But there was a man she didn't know there, a bricklayer with a cautious face and delicate white fingers, drinking a slow beer by himself before returning to the house he was working on down the street. This is a gentle man, she told herself. He followed her out to the street glass in hand.

"What happened to your face?" he wanted to know.

She handed him the jar of instant coffee. "Let me go with you," she said. The deep need in her voice surprised both of them. Afterward she never felt anything but grateful to the father of Maria de la Paz.

It was the time of her life she remembered with contentment, a time as close to peace as anything she knew. Gregorio the brick-layer took her in at his one-man stucco house in Fernando de la Mora, bought expensive medicines that did the burn on her face some good, sang her songs and played his guitar in the evenings when he came home from the construction site. Every day he told her the scar did not blemish her beauty, which was the clumsiest of lies, but she accepted the intention. And after a couple of weeks she joined him in bed.

Bed was the place where it finally went wrong, although at the time she did not understand why. She thought it went bad because it was in the nature of things that nothing could stay good. Sex with Gregorio was better than the repeated violations she endured with Don Andrés. Gregorio was respectful, and passionate, and reason-ably tender. But she felt herself rejecting steadfastly the sex itself and the pleasure it might have brought her. Not that she wanted to. Some days while he was away and she worked around the house, listening to the radio or teaching new words to his parrot, she thought about nothing else than how wonderful it was going to be the next time, that same night. But it was not.

She became pregnant, and the decency of Gregorio showed itself in the renewal of his passion as her belly swelled. The idea of her carrying his baby, he told her in a whisper under the covers, drove him wild with wanting. And Aramí thought the same must happen to her. But it did not, and Gregorio had no choice but to interpret her coldness as a rejection of him. She did not blame him. She was, after all, what the President would not abide—damaged goods. By the time the baby came she was sleeping alone on a cot in the little living room. Although the pride of fatherhood made Gregorio gen-erous, so that he invented every occasion to give her the chance to love him back, she found nothing inside she could pull out and offer him. When she closed her eyes to look what she saw was a blank field without depth, or measure, or color.

Pride made her leave Gregorio before he threw her out, pride and the urge to spare him the pain of separation from his new daughter.

One morning she kissed his lips with her own dry and feverish ones, a signal he caught but could not interpret. There was a little cash in the kitchen. He would have given her more if she had asked, so she felt no guilt in taking it. She walked away shielding the baby Pacita from the sun with a black umbrella she also took from Gregorio's house.

She walked a kilometer over sand and rough cobbles to the Avenida Eusebio Ayala, the *ruta,* a noisy confusion of shops and traffic that banged and people with business on their minds. She did not really expect to stumble into an easy solution, another Gregorio. She wandered slowly, aware of the picture she made: a tall, striking girl whose beauty was ruined by a large burn scar that covered her left cheek, a baby of eight months hugged to her breast. People stared. But that was the day she began to love Maria de la Paz. At Gregorio's she had wanted to love the baby, done a decent imitation of devotion to fool herself. It didn't work. As long as she stayed in the house the child was just the helplessly demanding effect of a cause she resisted, which was the surrender of her body to a force that blasted.

On the *ruta,* though, she felt the baby's fragile weight against her as something else, a live thing that needed cherishing, and hers alone. Even the ache in her arms after an hour's walking was pleasurable. She stopped every few minutes to wipe the sweat from Pacita's forehead, and she sang nursery rhymes she hadn't known she knew. The words came out of her mouth without any effort of memory; they were just there, and she thought the baby must be liking it from the way she wriggled, then snuggled against her. I'm a mother, she told herself. I'm your mother, she told the baby. It was new knowledge for both of them.

Afterward she could not remember the sequence of events that led to her being taken in as a temporary replacement for a household maid on a back street in Fernando de la Mora. Nor could she remember how long it was before the man of the house, who worked as a bill collector and slept with his briefcase chained to his bed, put his wife on the bus for Buenos Aires to visit her sister and came back to the house ready to rape Aramí. She remembered the struggle in the little room out behind the house where she slept, and Pacita crying as though she recognized the danger, and losing the struggle not because the bill collector was stronger but because her own weakness suddenly overwhelmed her.

She understood that too much remembering was not a profitable occupation for a woman in her circumstances. When events began to blur she let them go.

The father of Maria Carmen was an auto mechanic named Delicio whose wife was a garlic-sucking shrew who papered their bathroom walls with newspaper photographs of Julio Iglesias. Aramí stayed around Delicio for a year because he admired her body frankly and because he understood how to enjoy small things: half a bottle of wine, a story in the newspaper, a joke played on his neighbor. He lived skating on the surface of his own life, escaping when he could from an intolerable situation at home, but he had mastered the art of enjoyment, and she was willing to be his apprentice. They expected little of each other. Maria Carmen was a complication, but when she arrived Aramí loved her fiercely from the time the midwife placed her in her arms, having learned.

In 1989 the President was upended in a coup that brought democracy to Paraguay. When she heard the news Aramí regretted, perversely, that she had never met the man before he left for exile in Brazil. For a little while people hoped extravagantly that their lives would improve in ways that mattered, ways that could be measured. Then it became just a word, *la democracia*, one more weapon in the arsenal of those who were already heavily armed.

What Aramí wanted to happen under democracy was the obliteration by fire of the orphanage to which she had been delivered seven months before her first period: from the face of the earth, from the body of memory. And the public punishment of Don Andrés, now that the freedom to denounce evil existed. Every girl who had been under his charge would be allowed to lash his bare back once for every year she spent at the *guarderia*, and then the castoff women who taught the classes would have their turn. For a year or two she thought it might already have happened. She was not in a position to know much of what went on in Asunción. She was living in La Chacarita then, on the city's ragged edge, sometimes accompanied by the father of Maria Mercedes, who had worked as a driver until the company car he borrowed one night, with permission, was stolen. The thing that worked with Walter, the difference, was the sex. He must have had a story he would never tell her, because he was as skittish as she in bed, which for some reason made things easier for her, allowing her to learn, a little, to give and enjoy. When he was there. Then one day on a bench in Parque Caballero there sat Don Andrés, old and broken and ugly, meaning evil.

He was either retired or displaced, because she saw him there again, sitting or strolling listlessly, a man with too much time on his hands. She did not allow him to see her. She couldn't, because of the reaction each time that she could not control, losing her breath and trembling, going into a trance of anxious pain that didn't let up until he left or she sneaked away over the wall back home.

That was what democracy brought her.

Things were bad enough that a person might snap. In September Walter went to Buenos Aires to work in construction. But he had only sent money back twice, and both times it was less than she had thought it was going to be, the only explanation how high things were in Argentina so that even though a person made more money he spent more.

They were close to Christmas. During the day, to make a little money she stood with her girls at a traffic light downtown selling the long brown husks of *flor de coco* that people put in their houses for the holiday smell. The heat was unforgiving, like the penalty for a sin too big to be overlooked. It was worse, in a way, when a customer rolled down a window and she felt on her face the brief wave of frigid air escaping the car, a little bit of rolling heaven that made the heat of the street more closely resemble the hell imagined in the dreams of priests.

A person might snap, especially if she saw someone like Don Andrés on a bench unregenerate, unpunished, in his decrepitude enjoying the shade. Therefore Aramí was grateful for the messenger, who came back to see her several times in the next few days. The second time she appeared at night, when restlessness and the heat kept Aramí from sleep. She went outside to watch the river, on the black surface of which a lone pleasure boat with twinkling Christmas lights moved without sound. The woman wore the same white dress, radiated the same calm certainty she had in the park. Aramí admired her looks, felt complimented by them, since she knew they might have been her own, if things had turned out differently. You could kill him, the woman reminded Aramí. You could murder him and get away with it, you know. Aramí knew.

The woman did not always bring a message. Sometimes she didn't even speak. She was just there: on the streetcorner while Aramí hawked her fragrant *flor de coco*, on the tin roof watching her wash out clothes, on the dirt path that led to the store where they were tired of giving her credit but did anyway. Aramí didn't mind her silence any more than she minded the message. The quiet presence also comforted.

She thought she might go ahead and kill Don Andrés. It would be easy enough to manage, since he usually chose the siesta hour to visit the park, and often he was the only person there. She could overpower him and beat him to death with his own cane, then walk back home and finish her laundry. The tidy simplicity of the vision appealed to her. She would be acting on behalf of every girl who ever spent a night under the roof of the Guarderia Aramí.

The idea grew in her. She made sure she hiked up to the park every day at the siesta hour to lurk behind a eucalyptus and spy. He wasn't always there. The days he was not she regretted not having killed him the day before, when he was. Revenge was a sweet stone in her mouth that could be sucked on for a long time without the juice drying up.

Then Maria Mercedes wandered away again, which was what finally decided it for Aramí. There he was on a bench, inert and malevolent in the humid heat of early afternoon, unpunished, a stone toad. She knew her mind was made up by the fact that she did not lose her breath or go into a trance. Instead she watched him calmly as he watched Maria Mercedes play, stacking bottle caps in the dusty grass. His cane rested at an angle on the back of the bench. She wished that the messenger woman were there, for moral support, but that was too much to hope for.

She was running toward the bench. Then she had the cane in her hands. Its knobby wooden head gave the weapon a pleasant heft.

"Aramí," he said, startled but not yet afraid. "Look at me, I'm old." It was a confession, not a defense. His voice had the taste, and the smell, and the pulpy feel of rotten mango, something to be spat out.

She stood between him and the sun. His eyes in their skin pouches relaxed their squint. Maria Mercedes went on stacking bottle caps, humming a tune her mother didn't recognize. The urge to smash and disable the man grew stronger in Aramí. Up close, his features enraged her: the yellowed ivory hair, the hog-hide skin, the treacherous watery depth in the little eyes, the liver spots and trembling hands. The air he exhaled blew out thick through his nose, a brown crud expelled from the floor of his soul. That was probably only imagination but still true, one more ugly fact about the man.

He began to understand. His brain worked more slowly than it used to. "They killed the President, Aramí," he told her, a shield of tears forming in his eyes. "They killed him."

It was not true, of course. The President was in exile. But she understood what he meant. If he had said something else, anything but that, she would have been able to kill him. As it was the cane was suddenly too heavy to hold, and she let it drop into the dirt. Don Andrés didn't notice. His eyes were fixed in the middle distance at the spot where his dead president lay. That was when she began to laugh.

It was not a hysterical laugh, and not a laugh of desperation. It was a letting-go laugh, a spreading-out-and-settling laugh, a tickle on the deep inside that created a powerful sensation of pleasure in her body. The noise she made caused Maria Mercedes to look up from her game, and Don Andrés gulped, fishlike, in her direction.

She could not stop laughing. She gathered up her daughter, turning her back on the stone toad. The motion she made, simple as a knife slicing, made her feel even better. She looked around for the messenger woman, longing for one more sight of that unmarred beauty. She would have liked to ask her something: Did the perking-up pleasure make her feel this free, or was it the freedom that produced the pleasure? Not that it made any practical difference.

She hoisted her daughter on her hip and walked across the park, which wrinkled in the heat. In the evening *cigarra* bugs would make their wail, meaning watermelons were ripe in the countryside. She had saved one brown husk full of *coco* flowers for the house, on the off chance there was something to celebrate. As if she'd known. She hadn't. Before she climbed the fence down into La Chacarita she could smell the holiday, which was like one more way of saying *free*. She thought she would probably go on laughing.

two dead indians

Juan de la Cruz understood what a stroke was, and what it meant to be slipping away. The terror of dying was inside his body. That was to be expected. What took him by surprise was the strange and almost pleasurable sense of motion, of resisting and surrendering at the same time.

He needed time to think it through, but here came two Indians loping across his cotton field, rolling lightly on their bare feet as if they owned the place, or else they knew what they were coming for. They were Bolivians, no doubt about it. Their features were as clear and distinctive in the flesh as they had been in memory. All those years. The face of the taller one was narrow, long and sad, more openly expressive. The face of the squat one, by contrast, was a wooden mask hacked into human shape with a blunt knife by an untalented hand. You wouldn't see the anger in the mask, you had to guess at what was behind it. Both men had the same shining,

ruddy skin, and similarly restless black eyes, and longish, thick Indian hair that made Juan de la Cruz think of the Bolivian mountains down from which they'd come to fight in a war that had
nothing to do with them until it sucked them in, then spat them out
in a desert in which conscript soldiers drank their own blood and
piss to survive.

Juan de la Cruz himself had gone to the Chaco with no illusions.
The speeches and the songs were necessary, he supposed. Hard to
imagine a war without them. But they were only decorative. They
were the fringe on the saddle, nothing to do with the ride you took.
Their reasons to fight were not his reasons. In 1933 at age seventeen
he went into the desert to fight Bolivians because not going would
have branded him what he was not, a coward. When the officers
and the politicians and the feverish few who thought they had a
stake in the war whipped up the troops with images of treacherous
Bolivian devils he kept his mouth shut. He opened it to shout ¡*Viva
El Paraguay!* when they wanted him to shout it, but he knew the
war was being fought over territory and a dream of oil, and a few
men making more money than they already had. All of which skep-
ticism made what happened in the desert that much harder to explain, especially to himself.

The two Indians were coming in his direction but didn't seem to
be getting any closer. No hurry—not for them, not for Juan de la
Cruz Flor, who had no wish to die just because he was pushing
eighty. He felt sociable, hospitable in a maudlin, out-of-control way
that shamed him. He was eager to show the Bolivians his land, and
the life he had made putting things in and taking them out of it.
On the scales that judged that sort of thing you would naturally
think sixty years and more of unending honest labor would out-
weigh one unexplainable night in the desert. Probably you'd think
that, and probably you'd be wrong.

It was the right time of year for company: the hot middle of
March, the cotton so heavy on the plants the branches bent under
the strain. For once it was going to be a good year. You could tell

the good years with your fingers, the willing way the fruit let itself be stripped and dropped into the sack tied to your waist so that the motion was like a kind of eating, like stuffing yourself while food was there after a long period of doing without. He tried to lift his head out of the dirt to see what the Indians would see. Maybe he succeeded. Anyway he knew what was there: white cotton fruit in furred balls on green bushes in the sandy red earth rambling back to the woods, which blurred bluish in the late afternoon light. Pale green watermelons, hot to the touch, scattered like prizes around the field, their slender vines roping around the base of the money-bearing cotton plants. The neighborly thing to do would be to slice a ripe one down the middle, hand each Bolivian half a melon with a spoon and say, *Eat, this is the way we celebrate.*

Wishful thinking. The Indians were coming in his direction but not yet getting there. He tried to read the expression on the tall one's face but couldn't, quite. The other one was a mask, behind which only anger. There were some things that needed explaining. No, one thing. He was almost eighty years old. A lifetime of labor separated him from the war in the Chaco, or didn't. The terror of dying before the Indians got to him inflamed his outstretched body. He knew what a stroke was.

★ ★ ★

I can tell you're hearing me, Kai Juan, every last word. A priest, a good priest anyway, knows these things, because God wants him to know them. And I'm a good priest. Thus it is demonstrated: You're hearing me. I'm talking to you because I have a hunch God doesn't want you to die yet. It's too soon. You haven't shucked your burden yet. That's been evident to me for the past twenty-five years, plain as the nose on your face is how you'd say it in English. It's not true, by the way, that I'm forgetting my English. Mixing it up with the Spanish and the Guarani a good bit, I'll give you that. I can mangle three dissimilar tongues with dexterity and simultaneously, without regard for syntactical niceties or the squeamish ears of poets. *Pero de ninguna manera* I'm not forgetting my English.

Twenty-five years in Paraguay, if you can credit it. It's a long drive from Brooklyn, you will agree. Any idea what Brooklyn is like? 'Course not, why should you? I don't know the place myself anymore when I go back. Pai Patrick, you're a long way from the cotton fields of Paraguay; that's what I tell myself when I step off the airplane at JFK and contemporary North America rises up in its mantle of noise to grab me by the throat.

Attend, please, to this: My finger on your forehead is only an insurance policy. Extreme unction doesn't mean you have to die. If God wanted you to die He would not have sent me on my *motocicleta* past your field just now, would He? Your nephew Roberto happened to be nearby. He's been smitten lately with Don Justo's lovely daughter Primitiva, which is fine as long as they make a sacrament of their love, not just a festival of the flesh. That's what I told the boy, although he hasn't the ears to hear it. Anyway, I sent him to the *pueblo* on my bike for the doctor.

You're lying at the bottom of a deep well, my friend John of the Cross, and I don't have rope enough to get down to your depth, which is why all these words, hoping they have the weight to sink. The trick is to keep you interested until the doctor gets here.

I could do a better job if I knew your secret. What is it that's been torturing you all these years? I mean the specifics of your sin. Sin it must be, because nothing else has the staying power. It's complicated, you say? Maybe so, but the solution is simple. Ask for God's help to let it go. We're not ready to lose you, however. We'd love to have you around for the wedding of Roberto and Primitiva, which I intend to perform as soon as the pair of them are in the proper frame of mind. Their bodies have already decided.

It's my fault, isn't it, that you're out here alone. I know that. I'm admitting it, now, in your presence. I pushed you, and you snapped. I'm sorry. It's because of the way I am, which is naked. What I mean to say is that I am utterly vulnerable, as a person. I have no nerve endings. My nerves, and my consciousness, and my life itself are all mixed up with everybody else's. The door between me and thee, *vos y yo, che ha nde,* has somehow been left permanently open. I'm a separate person, of course, with tired legs and a white belly and an out-of-date doctorate in theology, but for reasons I have not yet fathomed no humanly devised fence can keep the who I am from climbing over and blurring into thee. This is a psychological thing. Few priests have it, thank God. Basically, I lack a firewall. I'm not sufficiently separated from my fellow human beings. And it's the connections that cause pain.

The result of this deficiency is that I can't help feeling myself what the people around me are meant to feel. Odd, is it not? It wears a body out. Just before I came by your field—my guilty conscience drove me out, and it was right—I experienced an overwhelming wave of your nephew Roberto's happy lust, and before that Primitiva's, which is different because it's mixed up with her triumph and her dim sense that love might be salvaged out of all the precariousness around her but probably won't be. And Don Justo's slow and hollow-headed anger that no one cares what he thinks about anything, least of all how his daughter marries.

What I have is a sickness I can no longer live without. It's what made me do what I did to you, Kai Juan de la Cruz. Does being sorry count?

* * *

There they were standing over him, crowding out the light, if there was any left to see by. The tall one glowered, demanding an accounting from Kai Juan. The short one with the mask face leaned over the Paraguayan cotton farmer, clenched his brown fists as though waiting for the word to strike. He smelled of onions, and leather, and wet wool, and the awful cleansing sweat that came out on a person in the grip of strong emotions. But there was something holding the two of them back, and Juan de la Cruz took advantage of the shield to order his thoughts.

Jimena, that was her name. Wide-shouldered and flat-chested, luckily enough, and tougher on the march than any three men in the regiment together. What she left back home and why she left it to fight Bolivians in the desert was a nut no one was going to crack. No discernible reason, either, that she picked Juan de la Cruz and Danilo to confide her secret in. Everyone else took her for the close-mouthed, knife-sharpening *hombre* she presented herself as. This was Pozo Envenenado. Not a place made famous by a battle, just an abandoned settlement in scrub-tree desert that their regiment was told to hold by higher-ups who had their reasons. The shacks were eaten up by the weather, which consumed everything in the Chaco, the way termites ate the wood that housed them.

She would not have asked them to run the risk of going for water unless she really needed it. To keep up the sham if for no other reason, although what man would begrudge a woman half a liter of water to clean herself during her period? Danilo said yes because he was restless even though they could have been shot for deserters if they were caught away from the regiment. Desertion was another way of saying common sense. Juan de la Cruz went along because he couldn't put into words the right reason not to go.

They thought the cloud cover made them safe, but before they reached the water hole a silent high wind ripped the clouds apart, exposing half a shining reddish moon that leered. Juan de la Cruz felt as vulnerable as he would ever feel in his life, which might go some of the uncrossable distance toward explaining but didn't. All his dreams were about water, all his fantasies, and all his practical intelligence was devoted to thinking about it. Thirst, he had thought at the beginning of permanent drought, acquired a smell of its own, but after the first week he understood it had twenty smells, thirty shades of dryness starting with parched, each to be suffered separately, separately survived. None of them had anything to do with songs and speeches. Briefly he felt like a hero, fetching water for a woman warrior.

Ironic that the moonlight they thought would give them away

gave them instead a glimpse of two Indians in Bolivian uniforms, momentarily careless, drugged by the water they also had left the security of their unit to find. Danilo signaled with his hand that he wanted to go back to their regiment at the settlement. The decision not to turn around belonged to Juan de la Cruz. A silly vision winged across the dry field of his consciousness: Latin American brothers in an impulse of solidarity sharing a canteen on the battle-field at night while nobody who cared was around to punish. Ridiculous. It was gone before it really arrived.

Why? was what interested Juan de la Cruz, what had always in-terested him. He left Pozo Envenenado to get water for Jimena, who needed to clean herself to stay sanely human in less-than-human circumstances. He did not turn around when Danilo wanted to turn around, because he could think about nothing that wasn't water, and because he was angry at the Indians who were keeping them away from it. Several whys there, but none of them was enough to explain anything.

Now, in his own cotton field, he had the impression that the Indians were talking to each other, almost certainly about him and what was to be done, although he was having a hard time making out their features, no longer distinct. He longed to know something he had longed to know forever: whether they were Aymara or Quechua. He'd been told both lived in Bolivia. Not that knowing would make any difference, but his ignorance chafed him. He was being mumbled over in his own cotton field in a language he didn't know the name of.

I can explain, he told them. The attempt to ward them off was pa-thetic; he knew it. But he needed time to straighten out his thoughts. He was beginning to confuse things: the complex smells of thirst in the Chaco with the homey smells of the squat Indian standing over him. Dreams about water with poor Jimena's voice running like water in a dry cave of memory. Indians in the field with Indians in the desert. Surrendering with resisting. A little time was what he needed.

* * *

I wouldn't jump to any conclusions about the doctor not getting here. Just to be on the safe side, though, I sent a little boy for an ox-cart. You shouldn't be jostled, but the way your breathing has slowed down . . . If worse comes to worse we'll load you on carefully and haul you to the schoolhouse. Sabina studied to be a nurse even though she wound up teaching.

I hope you have enough life left in you to forgive me.

The story goes that I was a passive kid, which my mother took for prototypical saintliness and my father the sign of a white liver. But they were both wrong. The fact of the matter is it took me years to learn to maneuver in the world with my deficiency. I had to erect some walls around me, without a clue as to what I was doing or why. You can imagine the cost. It helped that we were poor people, even though our sort of poverty was harder, in a way, than yours, because ours had to live elbow to elbow with such splendid wealth. Here at least Mother Earth protects you to a certain extent. You have no idea what growing up poor in rich America does to a person, except that in my case the experience helped turn the world into a bearable story.

As the curtain lifts, you see an Irish-minded woman on her knees and knuckles scrubbing the floors of the preoccupied upper-middle class. Eight children of various ages and temperaments and budding obsessions look wistfully out the windows of their rented house, listening rapt to the radio as though its musically encrypted messages, upon decoding, would give each of them what his heart requires, which is a way to someplace else. Offstage in speckled shadow, the woman's ne'er-do-well hubby stands smoking a Lucky Strike. He has traded his birthright belief in leprechauns for a blinding trust in luck—a secular vision of the state of grace if I ever saw one—that the ponies will run in the order he needs them to run in. And of course they seldom do, because God didn't want him to live in that sort of place.

The fifth child of the wistful eight is a passive kid, but the passivity cloaks a fierce ambition. He doesn't know it and wouldn't understand it if you drew it in single-syllabled pictures for him, but what he wants is to redeem the fallen world. To raise his mother from her swollen knees, send the old man to the racetrack in a late-model Buick and get him to lay off the Luckies, tuck little luxurious presents under the pillows of his sleeping siblings, wrapped in uplifting messages they cannot fail to understand. It's a big job, and the enormousness of it overwhelms the kid. He has no gift for making money, nothing to market to America. In desperation he turns to God, Who was waiting all along for him to make the right decision.

I'm tired of my own psychodrama, Kai Juan. It's as tedious as those horrible Venezuelan soap operas people in the *pueblo* are always watching. Don't let go of the rope I'm dangling down. The well is deep, isn't it? And don't go jumping the gun thinking the *médico* won't make it. It takes no time at all for God to forgive a sin. Will you be as quick to forgive me for driving you out here to die?

★ ★ ★

He was being carried, that much was for sure. And the *pitogüe* was making seductive, funereal noises in his ear. Which meant no one in the world thought he was going to make it. Probably they were right. He was being carried to his grave in the company of foreigners: two Bolivian Indians who didn't care how roughly they handled him, and a *yanqui* priest who didn't know how to let well enough alone.

The presence of the priest, if he was there, relieved Juan de la Cruz, because it meant that the Indians would take it easy on him. They might execute him—not much doubt they would, actually—but the death of Kai Juan de la Cruz Flor would be conducted with the respect and the restraint accorded rituals.

He wished he had one more chance to talk to Danilo. He had given up too easily after the disaster of the treasure hunt, and then the distance and the years got between them so there wasn't the ghost of a chance they could hold the one conversation they needed to hold. Ñeca must have had some kind of intuition. What do you want to go hunting buried treasure with a man like that for? she wanted to know. This was two, maybe three years after he married her, which happened in 1935 the same week he came home from the Chaco. She never met Danilo, and Kai Juan never talked about him, nor was she the kind of woman to say a blind no just to hear how it sounded coming out of her mouth. He wished she hadn't died, wished he could be sure she was somewhere waiting for him.

He took a bus to Villarrica, then rented a curly haired, dirty-white horse to get to Danilo's village in Guairá. The afternoon he showed up they got drunk together on cane whiskey and Danilo's wife Filomena got angry the same way Ñeca would have under similar circumstances. I've got a map, Danilo kept saying, though he didn't show it to him. They were lying on their backs in the darkness listening to the familiar racket of crickets and frogs. Juan de la Cruz wanted to ask his *compañero* whether the moon of the moment over Guairá was the same moon that had shown them the Bolivians at the water hole. But he didn't. Instead he listened to Danilo's treasure stories, which were more convincing than most because based on science more than greed. The map, apparently, was made by a soldier who had been there.

Back toward the end of the Triple Alliance War, marching toward death and immortality, Mariscal Lopez had jettisoned and buried enough wealth to make Paraguay what it once had been, the richest country on the continent. So far no one had found, or would admit to finding, the Mariscal's fabulous underground stash, which gained in value with every decade. It was difficult work that required superhuman patience, and it was dangerous. Apparently some sort of gas built up inside the chests, and sometimes that gas leaked out and up to the surface of the earth, where it was visible at night as a pale blue glow. When you found the chest, you had to cover your mouth with a cloth and rock the box with a stick several times to release the gas, which otherwise could be fatal; had been so to many, according to Danilo. He had a map, which was more than most had, and he had the patience, and both men had the need. When the *caña* wore off they fell asleep in a black pasture under the white eye of a new moon in a sky that wobbled.

But they woke up arguing. Over anything, everything. How to pack the horses. How much food to take, and what. How they'd split what they found; Danilo thought he deserved a higher percentage because the map was his. Hungover and prickly, they went at each other all morning. After siesta, Juan de la Cruz made up his mind. He told Danilo in plain words, "I'm not going treasure hunting with you." Neither man said a word to the other about what had happened at the water hole. Kai Juan mounted his rented curly horse and rode away alone. It was a long, mostly boring ride, long enough to do some slow thinking about what the idea of treasure had to do with the idea of oil, and either one of them with the idea of water. Not long enough, however, to come up with any right answers.

So there it was, the way it always had been: Two Paraguayan cotton farmers sneaking up in the desert dark on two Bolivian Indians—Quechuas or Aymaras?—drugged careless by the water that swelled their bellies like horses'. Close to the water hole, Danilo, damn him, gave them away with a noise. He stepped on a stick or something, which led to a vicious hand-to-hand fight notable for the absence of sound, as though none of the four was willing to admit he was there, away from his unit without permission.

The Paraguayans had surprise and momentum on their sides, though. Kai Juan knew they were going to win, never doubted it. What he remembered was tying up the Indians with a length of greasy rope he found on the saddle of their pack mule. His hand was bleeding badly. The short one with the ugly face had cut him with his knife, which was now stuck in the Bolivian's thigh. Finally some noise, when he rocked and moaned with the pain.

So fast to what would last. *"Ekiriri, nde tavy,"* Danilo insulted the moaning man in Guarani. No malice there. He only wanted to shut him up because of the way sound traveled across the flat, scrubby expanse of the Chaco night. The Indian said something back in his own language. Whatever it meant, it was strong. It was hate distilled, compacted, aimed at the Paraguayans with the force of a bullet. So fast, to what would last.

It was Juan de la Cruz who was at the throat of the squat, suffering Indian. He yanked the knife from his thigh, felt and rejoiced in the man's pain, waved the bloody knife in his face, letting out a spray of exploding noises that might or might not have been words until he noticed Danilo going at the taller Bolivian the same way. It was like competition, except not against each other. The knife went into Kai Juan's Indian's chest the way it would go into a melon; by chance he missed bone. So fast to two dead Indians.

That might have been all right, or tolerable, something you could live in the knowledge of and even sleep. They were in a war, and the dead men were their enemy. But the rejoicing, that began when Kai Juan felt the Indian's great pain as the knife came out of his thigh, started something in him that was like something also happening in Danilo that was like nothing that ought to happen ever to anyone. He looked at Danilo. In the marble moonlight the blood was black all over him, and his eyes were shining like a roasting saint's. The fever was not spent, not in either of them. Kai Juan remembered no words, no decision, just their fierce agreement, and the anger you couldn't call blind because it had its own eyes, which saw clearly what was there to see. Which was two wild and bloody Paraguayan cotton farmers slicing the Bolivians' penises off with the dead men's knives and shoving them down their throats. Two dead Indians. The blood was black. So fast.

Now, the anxiety was lifted from Kai Juan, almost suddenly. If he was going to be executed, so be it. He wanted to forgive the Indians the hard way they were handling him. He could take the hurt they caused him, although the pain in his trunk and in his limbs made it that much harder to think clearly when that was, above all things, what he required.

The bird still sang in his ear, fairly sweetly in a foreign tongue. If he could haven taken the priest's advice, to let it go, he would have. Years ago. But Pai Patrick's prayers missed the mark, never quite hit the target they were aimed at, which was the lightless place inside Kai Juan where what had happened in the Chaco settled and stayed, growing denser. He was going to his grave in the company of strangers, which was worse than going alone. Danilo, he remembered, died young, in 1975. His wife Filomena sent word that he was gone, along with a message: Not his fault. Maybe it wasn't.

★　★　★

God lift the stone from your heart, Kai Juan. How presumptuous the words sound to me, now. Yesterday, sitting in your patio, I thought they were the earnest of my good intentions. Commend your sin and your soul to God, I told you, and He will lift the stone. I should have known something was wrong when you wouldn't look back at me. You kept your eyes fixed on that *pitogüe* in the lemon tree as though the bird was the only thing in the world that mattered to anybody.

Lift him gently into the cart, neighbors. He's still breathing, but only for a little while longer. There's no doctor in town. He went to the city for a checkup, they tell me, after a week of angina pains. Not that there's anything he could do if he were here.

It's this strange disorder of mine, Kai Juan, that pushed me to push you to confess your secret sin. I have felt your transgression as though it were mine, ever since I've known you, even though I don't know what it is you've done that could haunt you so all these years. And I kept leaning on you even after the *pitogüe* flew off and you still kept staring at the lemon tree. I told myself it was God working through me, his dented vessel, to draw the sin and the pain out of you. And maybe it was. But if it was, I spoiled it.

All these years in Paraguay, and still to make the same mistakes. I'm reduced to elegy. God bless the huge, high rolling wheels that bear our neighbor, Juan de la Cruz, veteran of the Chaco War, and the dust the wheels raise, and the sweaty, muscular backs of the oxen hauling and their pseudointelligent black eyes, and the bare brown feet of the children who can't help thinking this is like a celebration of some kind, and maybe it is or should be, and the sons and daughters who cry because their imaginations are traditional and insufficiently exercised. And the soul of the wife who was impatient and went on ahead. And the lust of Roberto and Primitiva, hidden in this crowd of grievers because they think they have to hide it, that it be converted into love by the action of grace and their own conscious effort.

God lift these stones.

*   *   *

About time. They were letting him down. Less roughly than he would have expected. Easing down, being eased, he smelled leather and onions and wet wool and that dangerous sweat, which together meant Bolivian Indians in the Chaco at a water hole near Pozo Envenenado on an erratically cloudy night, which meant what it meant. There was no more singing in his ear. They were alone, finally, the three of them. He struggled to make out the features on their faces. Features could be read, and he assumed they had something to communicate to him.

Although maybe they didn't. Maybe the fact that they were there with him was all, and enough. The idea that that could be true made him giddy with hope, for a moment. Then an odd thing: a sense of being abandoned unjustly when he realized the Indians were walking away from him, leaving him behind. He was hurt, devastated. He wondered where they had dumped him. Were they still in his field? He tried to lift a handful of dirt with one hand, wasn't sure he did, or could. And then wanting to go with them. I'm sorry, he called out to their vanishing backs. He didn't think it would do much good. They did not stop walking or even turn around to look back at him. There was no reason to feel this good, but he did. He allowed himself to rest.

the telemachus box

Damaso del Campo

was looking for a way to die.

"An authentic gesture?" That was how Nancy Schmidtke put it, the words she chose: *un gesto auténtico*. Except that she was talking about Rigoberto and the way he had elected to die, or been elected. Damaso supposed that he should be careful in her company.

"This conversation doesn't interest me," he told the North American woman who had tracked him down. Not that he was in hiding. It was more of a straight-on sentence than he tended toward, a form of courtesy toward a foreigner.

He had not known that he was looking for a way to die until she showed up and told him she was writing a book about his poetry. That explained some of the enmity he enjoyed feeling.

"What kind of press is going to want to do a book on the poetry of Damaso del Campo?" he thought he wanted to know, moved by an old impulse of vanity that sometimes resembled pride. Sometimes it was pride itself. But as soon as he asked the question he lost interest in the answer. The University of California. So what?

"But don't you think it was perfect?" she probed. "A poet who has written the last thing he is going to write, and knows it, joins an expedition to rescue a comrade who has been kidnapped by thugs. The thugs are in the pay of a nasty individual who is responsible for the murder of striking workers. The comrade investigates the murders and disappears. The only way for him to appear again is by the poet taking the bullet that kills him. It's like . . . What is it? It's like the last authentic line the poet speaks, and it certifies all the lines that he has spoken before it."

Cuate, the mynah bird, erupted in angry syllables when she stopped.

"You know, I can't make out a word of that bird's Spanish," Nancy Schmidtke admitted. She disliked conceding defeat. Damaso saw that facet of her character revealing itself early. He was not sure whether he admired or despised it.

"Keep listening," he encouraged her. "It will come to you."

Because of the heat, they were sitting in the little living room of the house he was renting in the town on the Caribbean coast outside of which his mother was buried. His sisters and brother were all in Tegucigalpa, where they led lives that had little to do with the fishing village of their common birth. There were a few incurious cousins in la Fiera, and an uncle, blind at ninety, who lived alone in a dirt-floored shack. Tío Tomás was waiting for his comrade Jesus to come striding across the green surface of the sea in big boots to take him where he belonged, which was someplace better. But, like his siblings, Damaso had made his life elsewhere, so that la Fiera was not so much the home to which he returned as a differently configured exile, one more variation on the theme he knew how to hum.

He had whitewashed the walls of the little house, inside and out, when he rented the place, vigorous action praised by his neighbors, who watched, thought they might do the same to their own houses any day now. When they passed him in the street or came to the door selling bananas or oranges or fresh-caught fish, people addressed him as *Poeta*. He liked the old-fashioned respect therein betokened. It confirmed him publicly in his office and identity, legitimate as any engineer they called *Ingeniero*, any doctor. But he had hung nothing on his whitewashed walls: no mementos or memorabilia, certainly not the citation that accompanied the decoration the government of France had awarded him. One wanted his walls white, and the bird in the cage black, the sand a sandy color and the sea whose verge it made sea colored, which was to say never the same color twice in a row no matter how frequently one looked out at it.

"Our father was a fisherman here," he told Nancy Schmidtke. That much was easy to say.

"You were close to Rigoberto," she prodded, "weren't you? You were together at Patrice Lumumba in Moscow."

And in Havana, Rigo was the one who sat up all night with Fidel in the beach house talking poetry and politics and the imagination of Garcia Márquez. Damaso may or may not have been invited. A certain sequence of events had blurred in his memory. What was left was an aftertaste of bitter. Rigoberto had owned something Damaso was smart enough to know could not be faked, or learned, or stolen. In the morning, he gave Damaso the handful of cigars Fidel had sent him away with. He went to bed whistling. Waiting in the bed was a Cuban woman with long brown legs who spoke in unintended couplets.

"Rigoberto is a fine poet, perhaps a great poet," he told the North American woman.

"Of course he is. So is Damaso del Campo. At a certain point it comes down to taste. I happen to like the poems of del Campo better, a good deal more, than those of his countryman."

"No accounting for taste," he agreed. "There's lemonade in a pitcher out back in the kitchen. It's not cold. I have no ice."

"It doesn't have to be cold. Wet is enough."

"There's rum to pour into it."

"Rum would be fine."

She excused herself formally to go to the kitchen, a detached room behind the house where he spent almost no time. He was minimizing.

She was blond, fading to a shade of brown that he approved of. She was forty-five, or close to it. Her breasts were large. There was a particular roll in them as she moved, an identifiable motion re-flexed in the whole body that managed to soothe and evoke simul-taneously. He felt saliva secreting in his mouth, a pleasurable thirst, like memory unbidden.

Ilyana, that was who she reminded him of, his official Russian translator. Back when back then. There was no longer need for irony, political or any other sort, in the resemblance. What counted was the similarity itself, the same slow roll in the body, the same radiant weight.

Ilyana slept with him because she thought doing so would im-prove her translation of his work. It was an experiment that chal-lenged her constitutional caution. Showing up in his room with a bottle of plum brandy and a single red hibiscus—God knows where she got her hands on it, what it cost—she quizzed him on the nuances of half a dozen strictly Honduran words he favored in his poems. His assigned room was tiny, suffocating. Sitting on the bed, Ilyana took notes. Her body betrayed her, clumsiness making grace, almost light.

In bed with him, under covers, she had tried to liberate herself from her mind, her sense of civic duty, her scruples regarding adjec-tives. In the dour Moscow winter she made heat for which he was grateful. If he had had something insightful to contribute about his poetry he would have offered it up in praise and thanks, a consola-tion prize for her attempt to transcend herself. He gave her the nothing he had.

Nancy Schmidtke served him rum-laced lemonade, and they sat like opponents taking a time out in weathered, canvas-bottomed chairs in the doorway, where a small breeze flickered and returned. Her facility with Spanish was a minor goad. In Moscow, Damaso's Russian had not gone beyond restaurant basic; in Paris, his French was scarcely better. In Iowa, after four full semesters of diligent engagement with English words, he remained outside the language. But there were lots of Nancy Schmidtkes. They had shown up in droves during the early eighties, looking for something specific and true to which to attach their allegiance. That was the best they could do in the face of their government's perfidy; the unjust war shamed them. All those M-16s, those rocket launchers, all that suborning. They were grim parsers, finding political allegories wherever they turned their high-intensity gaze. Without wanting to, they unmanned the Latin lovers they took.

"Tell me something," she said. She needed an opening, a way in. "Anything at all. Anything about anything."

"I am completely indifferent to your book," he told her.

She nodded. It was what she expected.

"Now you tell me something," he said in his inadequate English. There was no chance she would switch out of Spanish. Talking to the poet of her preference, she would permit no filters.

"When I was seventeen I got pregnant. I didn't want to marry the father, so I raised my son alone."

"Why didn't you want to marry the man?"

"The way he brushed his teeth turned me off."

Damaso nodded, sipped his lemonade, listened to Cuate's turgid muttering behind them. In the street outside, a monumental black pig with stiff bristles kicked up dust, fretted by a yellow dog with bent ears. The dog's enthusiasm was a sham. Farther away, someone was practicing the violin part to a *ranchera* he had always detested, "*El Rencór del Débil.*" It was a song about not. He had heard it too often. The violin notes were tentative, like thoughts not half formed.

"I'm going to write the book. I have the contract. Are you willing to talk to me?"

"I have nothing to say."

"I'll ask you questions. You can answer them. That's all there is to it. I'll assume from the outset that your responses are wily and many layered."

"What are you going to call your book?"

"Something with Telemachus in the title."

"I was afraid of something like that. Hey, what did the bird just say?"

She turned to the corner where the cage hung from a hook. The bird hushed. "Sorry, I didn't catch it. You know, I didn't expect you to be interested in my idea, Damaso."

"I'm not." It was really quite enjoyable to speak simple direct sentences and mean them. He had lost the art, or the habit.

"Okay, here goes: I think, no, I know that you are Spanish America's Telemachus. You're the man of honor who is always setting out on a dangerous journey to find out what happened to his father. You're always looking, aren't you, for the consequential thing that has been lost. Your father disappeared on the Caribbean."

"He was out fishing. He happened to go alone that day. There was an accident. No mystery."

"They never found any trace of his boat. There was no storm. There was talk."

"There's always talk. Talk is how people entertain themselves here."

"I didn't expect you to buy any of this. I just figured I owed you a straightforward explanation before we begin."

"We're not beginning."

But he was wrong. They were, in fact, beginning. Her patience was the most insidious form of persistence. She rented a room a block away from his. She cooked things he liked to eat, washed his dishes. She moved her body in his vicinity with a natural self-assertion that poor Ilyana in Moscow had not imagined possible, so she did not even try pretending. Once, for no discernible reason, Schmidtke took a small mirror from her leather purse and applied a line of lipstick to her lips, which were full, a pale brown at the puckering edges, a wondrous mobile cave from which to emit syllables in Spanish or English.

When she had closed the cover on the mirror and returned it to her purse, she told him, "I understand that you have envied Rigoberto. The reception that people gave him, that easy acceptance. All the romantic dash. And then the final gesture of his death, saving a friend who needed saving. I understand that perfectly, and I have no interest in using it against you. It never got into your poems. For me it's not relevant."

On the second morning of her stay, he asked her to walk with him down to the beach, where he threw her mini-cassette recorder into the water, which was momentarily the color of copper. They watched it quickly sink. Midmorning, the beach was deserted. The only boat in sight lay upside down, a hole half a meter round punched in the stern.

"There is one thing," she warned him, shading her eyes with cupped hands to scan the surface of the sea as if to be sure that her little machine wasn't going to float. "One thing I do have to pry into. It has to do with what you were thinking and feeling when you decided to come back to la Fiera."

"There's a woman up that way who sells coconut milk." He pointed. "She keeps it in a refrigerator. It's cold." It was as close as he came to an invitation. He wanted to make sure she understood what he was not offering.

He was not willing to tell her how it happened. Telling would reveal a poverty of spirit he preferred to keep for himself. Anyway it was not a decision. Decisions called for a willed consciousness to do a thing, or not to. Coming back to la Fiera and the beach and the sea-colored sea in which his father had disappeared was nothing willed.

On the third anniversary of Rigoberto's death, the French Embassy had organized a tribute dinner at which they invited Damaso to speak. The French had discovered high policy value in publicly lauding the cultural contributions of antiimperialist men of letters in the Caribbean Basin. Damaso supposed that their disappointments in Africa were at the back of it. Events like Rigo's dinner were an efficacious way to thumb their noses at the North Americans, in the giant's very shadow, as it were. And in the case of Rigo, little reconstructive surgery was needed to make him over into Central America's most eloquent decrier of imperialist push. It was there in the poems just as it had been in the man: imbedded in tissue fiber, bile in the liver, microscopic beasties in the blood.

Damaso spoke sparingly at the dinner, celebrated in the residence of the French ambassador. He chose, instead, to read from Rigo's poems. Now that Rigo was dead, he found himself a better reader of his friend's work. The absolute distance helped.

Two days after the dinner, a small story describing the event ran in *Tiempo*. The story quoted the word *revolución* coming out of Damaso's lips. There was no context. So he was not surprised to get a call from a colonel in intelligence.

"Why don't you stop by my office?"

Damaso stopped by. The office was bare in a style he approved of. The walls were painted a pale martial green. The colonel's desk was tidy, the papers in one neat sheaf. A banana lay next to the telephone, which was a complicated, up-to-the-minute machine that performed, Damaso assumed, numerous useful functions. A mynah bird dozed in a cage behind the desk.

"I didn't have to come by," he told the colonel. "Times have changed."

The man he addressed was fifty at most. Fifty seemed impossibly young, a millennium away from the poet's sense of place and space. Everything about the colonel was militarily crisp, a quality Damaso also appreciated. The man's close-cut hair shone silver.

"Of course you didn't have to come by," he agreed. "I read the piece in *Tiempo*."

"Of course you read it."

"Reading it made up my mind for me."

Damaso waited. He preferred not to prompt unless he had to. The silver colonel swiveled his hair in the direction of a file cabinet from which he pulled a folder that had to be labeled del Campo/ Damaso: 19 something to 19 something else.

"Here it is," the colonel waved it at him. "Everything the government ever obtained about the poet del Campo. Some of the things in here may actually be true, who knows?"

He spread the file open in front of him on the big desk, thumbed through it purposefully, fastening on a report that drew his eye. "In nineteen seventy-nine," he asked, "did you collaborate in the movement of a shipment of some Czech rifles from Nicaragua to the FMLN in El Salvador?"

"Nineteen seventy-nine was the year the Sandinistas took down Somoza, wasn't it?"

"I believe that was the year."

He shook his head. "Must have been some other poet."

"I didn't think so." The colonel shook his head. "If you know what to look for, the inventions are easy to spot. These sorts of fabrications have served their world historical purpose, however; some would say that, wouldn't they? At any rate, after I read the article in the paper, I pulled out your file and looked at it carefully, and something happened to me."

Prompting was called for. "What happened?"

"A crisis. Not a crisis of conscience." Elbows on the desk, he brought the tips of his fingers together in a gesture that minced. Damaso decided he liked the man. "It was different. It was more like a crisis of faith. This is ludicrous, is it not?" he wanted to know, slapping the file folder, which he had closed.

Damaso agreed that it was ludicrous.

"The things a person can do are limited. I recognize that. But I'd still like to do something. Here, take it. Take the whole damn thing. It's the only copy. You'll find it entertaining reading."

As he lifted the file, the mynah bird stirred and spoke. What came out was a muddy stream of gibberish.

"I'd rather have the bird," Damaso told the colonel.

"What?"

"The bird." He pointed.

"You don't care what's in here? It's your life. It's a twisted, distorted version of your life. These are your lies, *Poeta*."

"I'd rather have the mynah."

"Then take it," the colonel told him. He returned the file folder to the cabinet, and Damaso walked out of the office with the cage under a heavy fabric shroud.

It was not the colonel's bird. The mynah had belonged to the ambassador from Paraguay. There had been a misunderstanding. Not a scandal, because no one was surprised, let alone outraged. The misunderstanding had to do with the terms under which the ambassador was bringing duty-free Mercedeses into Honduras and re-selling them. He had failed to spread a sufficient amount around. There was confusion, and he decided to abandon his post. Some personal possessions were left behind.

One of the possessions the departing ambassador did not claim was the mynah, which spoke only in Guarani, Paraguay's indigenous language. Outside Paraguay no one understood Guarani. Damaso thought he could teach the bird to speak Spanish. The colonel had not seriously tried, content to let the bird shower him with words and phrases that sounded prophetic, or menacing, or seductive, according to the listener's frame of mind.

Damaso made arrangements to leave Tegucigalpa and return to his boyhood home in the north coast as though Cuate was all he had lacked to put the plan into motion. Although he had not given up, he had not been able to coax a single Spanish word from the bird.

Eventually he decided that Nancy Schmidtke was not really like the energetic North American women who had taken over Central America in the war years. Although she had a ready grasp of the politics of Damaso's world, the impulse that drove her was aesthetic. It had to do with words, and the connection between words and the world they stepped on. He learned, over time, that she loved his poems. She recited many of them from memory, and her Spanish was good enough that listening produced pleasure. Best, perhaps, she was willing to give as well as take. Her openness, which came out in the stories of her life, was not calculated, not a tactic intended to draw him out in response. She was the most unforced creature he had met.

It cost him to walk. He had the sense that he was walking time off his life. But he would not deny himself the pleasure of walking in la Fiera, and on the beach, and in the green-clogged countryside, in the company of an intelligent woman who loved his life's work. So they walked. And she cleaned and cooked. Sometimes she sang, always in English; they were fragments of rock-and-roll tunes. Her singing voice was deeper than her speaking voice, as though the music exposed a depth she herself was not aware of.

"In 1969 I lived in a commune in Northern California," she told him.

"You were a hippie."

"Not strictly speaking. I was very young. I took lots of LSD. By myself, in the woods at night a long way from where we were living. One time God appeared to me in the woods. That's what I thought. I thought it for a long time, for years."

When he began to talk back, what he had to say disappointed both of them. The well was dry.

"Not dry," she insisted. "The water table has dropped, that's all."

But all the things he found to say were dry. They were pieces, some with sharp edges, as of something dropped. Or they were threads, dry and brittle to the touch, plucked things from a fabric with no give. His work, he understood with a slow surge of panic, had wasted him. He was gone into the words he had put on pages. He was reduced to anecdotage.

"Patience," Nancy Schmidtke counseled him. "*No tengo nada de prisa. The longer I stay, the safer I'll feel.*"

"Why safe?"

"Before I go home I want to be sure I won't go back to the man I was living with."

"Why don't you want to go back to him?"

"It has to do with the way he eats his eggs."

She was telling the truth. That helped. But the panic surged, however slowly. One night he put his hands on her face. He traced its lines, found the cracks and canyons there. He felt the flesh that gave and the bone that didn't.

"Ten years ago I would have been honored to make love with you."

She kissed his eyes, his cheeks, finally his mouth. "Ten years ago, Damaso, I wasn't ready for you. Timing is destiny, or do I mean that destiny is timing?"

She brought rum and lemonade, and they sat in the back patio in a homey sprawl of bushery and untended fruit trees until the sun set.

That night he had the dream. It was the emotion of distant wanting that Nancy Schmidtke's face had evoked in him. He seldom remembered his dreams anymore, but this one was worth the recall. There was a waterfall in woods. Nearby on flat rocks a woman sat, too vigilant to be at rest. She had the head of a bird, and wings that looked as though they were made of copper: thin burnished feathers like leaves against the frame of sinew.

Several things happened in the course of the dream. There was digging in a hole, and water running, and the simple visual delight of the waterfall and the woods and the bird woman. What mattered, however, was what he came out of the dream with.

The box. How could he have forgotten the box? That was why he had returned to la Fiera, although he hadn't known that when he acquired Cuate and came home. He got out of bed. It was the middle of the night. Something that was not a clock ticked. He was remembering now. Off the coast—several kilometers out if he had it right—there was a small island. Too small for anyone to live on. He remembered coconut trees, hermit crabs scuttling, a ring of coral in the water below, and bright colored fish appearing and disappearing like God's evanescent thoughts. They called it la Pequeñita, the Little One. That was where he had buried the box. How could he have forgotten?

Outside, someone had left a shovel leaning against a shed wall. He took it.

On the beach, he had his pick of boats to borrow. No one was going to begrudge the poet the loan of his boat. Honor attached to the request, to the concession. He chose the smallest craft in sight, *la Voluntad*. Hauling the boat across the sand, he was sure he heard Nancy Schmidtke behind him, calling his attention to something. He stopped, listened hard until he realized the place from which she was calling was not behind him, not out there anywhere. It was not a place that could be located. Not from any sense of duty but because he wanted to play, he took the time to draw with a stick some lines in the sand that a properly perceptive woman would interpret as thanks. He hoped that she would see them before morning traffic and the tide erased his message.

The boat moved easily in the water, although the strain of leaning on the oars told on him before he was ten minutes gone. That didn't matter. He paced himself. There was no hurry. A small spot of pain appeared in the small of his back, like an invisible stain. Something close to half a moon rode low in the sky, but there were few clouds. After a few minutes, Damaso was able to make out the stars. Once, resting his shoulders, he saw a meteor flash.

The preposterous thing was he could not remember what was inside the box. Thanks to the dream, he remembered burying it. He remembered sand grating between his toes on la Pequeñita, and digging the hole. He thought he remembered—although his mind had always been high spirited and willful, with an independent sense of sport—placing the rectangular green metal box in the hole he had dug. But he could not for the life of him remember what was in the box.

He aimed his borrowed boat in the direction he was sure the island lay. Patience, that was what Nancy Schmidtke was always saying. It will come. He rowed steadily, rested when he had to. Resting, he studied the stars. He had also forgotten how closely remoteness resembled majesty. How was it that a person forgot such basic things? There was less wind in his lungs than he would have wanted, but he was an old man. The stain of pain in the small of his back was spreading. He felt it creep and grow. It didn't matter.

His principal worry was the light. There was no reason to fear it, but he dreaded being seen out on the water by someone from la Fiera, by anyone from anywhere. But it would be foolish to push his body, so he continued to row steadily, and to rest when he had to.

The moon went down. The stars were splendid. The water was black. He rowed. Eventually, he saw the sky lighten in the east. That discouraged him, as did the pain in his body, which was now fierce. The light came gradually. He was pleased to observe no boat in view. Nothing. Although he was certain he was going in the right direction, there was as yet no sign of la Pequeñita.

A gull lit on the gunwale of *la Voluntad*. It was perfectly white, whiter than gulls usually were; unblemished. The bird stayed put, wings tucked, its eyes scanning the sea and the low sky. Damaso was relieved that there was nothing human about the eyes, there was absolutely nothing unbirdlike.

He had to rest. Although still no sign of the island. He lay back in the boat until he found a position of rest in which his back hurt a little less. His hand found the pole of the shovel he had lifted and wrapped itself around it. It was remarkable that the gull stayed perched where it did. It was just as remarkable that he had forgotten what was buried in the box on the island.

He worried, when he could focus, about drifting, about losing the position he had gained with all that rowing. But he could not always worry. Watching the gull on the gunwale soothed the eye. He was not quite ready for the sides of the boat to fold out the way they did, but they folded out, and he accepted the change as a good thing. He was impressed by the color around him. The color might have been the sky. The number of things a person forgot. He wanted to believe lost things were there for the digging up. It was an article of faith.

He was moving across a wide, flat space of conspicuous colors, which shimmered as they shifted. Movement was the cause of the shifting. There was a word for that movement. Inexorable. Not a word a person forgot. Against the planes of color, he noticed, the gull's white gleamed.

mengele dies again

Mid-March, before the infernal summer heat subsided, a brusque, elderly man wearing doctor's whites appeared in Potrerito, an isolated village of poor cotton farmers in southern Paraguay. They said his eyes were mean. Advertising himself to his new neighbors as a specialist in natural healing, he moved into an abandoned shack near the village center. From the beginning he was disliked by the people of Potrerito, who found him *antipático*. Nevertheless, when they saw that he was indigent the director of the school organized a system whereby nearby families took turns bringing him his meals. Also from the beginning, the man berated and abused those who brought him his food, especially the children. By the end of his first week among them, the villagers were calling him Mengele.

He was only in Potrerito, he explained to the school director, because of his vision.

The school director was a Christian spinster who had given her adult life to exorcising ignorance among the humblest of the humble, farmers who worked their small fields of cotton by hand, living and dying in isolation. "You're a sinner," she told Mengele, "and you're not well. You must confess your sins." Rudely digging into the plate of simple food she had brought him, between mouthfuls he summarized for her the vision that had driven him to Potrerito from whatever hideout he had abandoned: There was no such place as within. All that existed was surface, what you saw. Truth was only recognition of the visible, it was what you garnered from observing the brute collision of opposing exteriors.

"My life's work," he told her.

She waited for a verb that didn't come. She was a perceptive, disciplined woman who read John of the Cross and Augustine for the company they gave to her solitude. "What about your life's work?" she insisted.

He looked at her with the coldly curious eyes with which men often appraised women. His white hair had the sheeny yellow cast associated with infirmity, but the impression he gave her was of bullheaded vigor. Pilar, *la señorita directora*, was fifty. She understood that her attractiveness was based on an illusion: Even to those who didn't know her she seemed sweetly virginal. She was, to the world, an unplucked fruit. What no one knew was that there had been a man, years ago, in another part of Paraguay. She lived comfortably in the memory as inside a small house whose walls were made of pleasure.

Mengele gnawed a yellow stick of boiled manioc root, closed his eyes tightly. For the duration of the pain spasm she did not exist. "Everything I've done," he told her softly when he came back to himself, "was done in the service of truth."

"And now?"

"And now I've had a vision that showed me the folly of my life's crusade. I tried, you see, to penetrate to the heart of things, to the secret core of life itself. Through science. Through objectivity and experimentation. My mistake was in believing that there was such a secret core. Because of course there is not."

"There is a Polish priest in the *pueblo*, a missionary. I will tell him you wish to confess."

He cursed her in serviceable Guarani, the country's private language, which the farmers of Potrerito preferred over Spanish. But his accent was horrible; it grated on her educated ear. He thrust the empty plate at her, closed the door to his shack muttering in what she presumed was German.

People believed that bad luck lived in the house into which Mengele had moved. Two rooms with dirt floors and a thatch roof that leaked, it had been built years earlier for the *comisario*. One room had served as his office, the other a cell. During one of the few times the cell had been occupied, however, its inmate was murdered. Locked up for rustling a single cow, he was shot in the head while he slept by a man whose sister the rustler had reportedly seduced. Later, after the *comisario* had abandoned the place, an American Peace Corps volunteer had moved in. The American lasted a year. He cleared out in the middle of one moonless night, no explanation, after the neighbors heard the sounds of a foreign woman crying and laughing and then screaming hysterically from inside the house. It was the only dwelling in the village a man like Mengele could have chosen to inhabit.

He called himself Dr. Jorge Navarro. Navarro was perhaps the most common surname in the area. Periodically he would go through a little show of finding some pretext to haul out from the pocket of his pants his identity card, which showed a picture of the doctor looking slightly younger, slightly healthier, slightly more aggressive. Juan Navarro Benitez was indeed the name printed on the I.D. card, but no one in Potrerito believed the transparent lie. Anyone with ingenuity and a little cash could obtain documentation proving he was anyone, including Adolph Hitler if that was what a person required.

The more moderate April weather seemed to do Mengele some

good. He left his shack more frequently. Wearing a broad-brimmed straw sombrero, in the early morning hours he strode purposefully through the village and back into the still wild woods that surrounded Potrerito. The forest in that part of the country, he told people, sheltered plants whose medicinal properties and powers were truly extraordinary. That much they believed. They had been curing themselves with roots and bark and leaves forever. And they believed he must know something about the science of healing. Or something, anyway, about the human body. They had heard stories.

And they were curious. The children, especially, liked to dog him wherever he went, staying just out of reach of his hard balled fists, which he was eager to use on any child who threatened the circle of privacy he worked to keep around him. They loved hearing him curse them out in his unmusical Guarani. Television had not yet reached Potrerito, and people remained each other's principal entertainment.

"Don't ever do that again," Mengele told *la señorita directora* after the Polish priest showed up to confess him. She understood it was a threat, wondered what he might conceive doing to her. He had come out of the woods with a straw basket heaped with medical treasure: the same roots and bark and leaves the villagers used, a herd of kids behind him as usual. The priest, a florid man with a silver-tipped wooden crucifix around his sunburnt neck, was sitting cross-legged in the grass in front of the shack reading from his breviary. Not even Pilar learned what happened between the two foreigners when Mengele invited him inside his house. After twenty minutes of wrangling in a language nobody eavesdropping could understand, the Polish priest stormed out of the shack and left the village on his red Japanese motorcycle.

For those watching him carefully, the visit of the priest appeared to affect Mengele for the worse. A mark was notched on the calendar of his decline. He spent less time in the woods, more idle hours in the shade cast by the walls of his house, especially out back where a well had been dug. It was only a hole in the ground, but the water was sweet, and Mengele was frequently observed casting down a small tin bucket, pulling up cool well water and drinking it, dousing his overheated German-type face, washing and washing again his hands and arms and neck, sponging his flat-nailed feet.

And reading. It was obviously a rare, expensive book, bound in dark blue leather, thick as the Bible. Marisol, who lived at the school with Pilar, sneaked a look at the book once when she was delivering Mengele his supper. It wasn't in Spanish, and she was reasonably sure what she saw wasn't German, either. The text was written not with letters but with some sort of exotic characters. He had filled up all the white space in the margins with comments of his own, using the same strange characters that could have been magic runes for all anybody in Potrerito knew.

Pilar made sure she herself took him a meal at least once a week. The bile in the man fascinated her. The hostile anger that never quite boiled over, or boiled away, offended her sense of propriety, which was liberally Christian and influenced by thirty years of village life, which forced a person to make what she thought of as civilized accommodations. She studied his face, took a bus to Encarnación on the border with Argentina, defined by the mighty Paraná River. She spoke with a teacher friend there, who sent her to a dentist in the muddy neighborhood built by contraband near the bridge to Posadas. The old newspaper pictures the dentist showed her were not quite conclusive, but they came close.

"All those Nazis left Germany with a poison tooth," he told her.

She didn't understand.

"A hollow tooth," he explained, "with poison in the hollow. They were supposed to take the poison if it ever came to the worst. I guess Mengele decided the worst was over. Ten years ago, eleven at the most, I pulled that tooth and replaced it with a normal false one."

"If you knew he was Mengele, why didn't you report him to the authorities?"

He looked at her wondering whether she was naive or only cunning. "If I had known a Jew, maybe I would have. But I'm not ashamed to tell you I was afraid to do much. Those people have long arms."

On the long ride back to Potrerito *la señorita directora* wondered why she herself was doing nothing to report the man to someone who cared. She disliked him as much as anyone else in the village, took an uncommon, unchristian satisfaction from seeing him limp through his desperate, dead-end days. The world's best revenge, it may have been, was his living long in the condition he was in.

The night she returned to the village she was disturbed by a dream. She was wandering around inside that same house of memory, her hands blindly, obsessively feeling the walls of pleasure that closed her in. But there was someone, an intruder, in the house. She knew she ought to leave, but she did not want to move away from those comforting walls.

When the strength of the sensation woke her she listened to a cock crowing in the insect-ridden black, reminded herself that reason was a legitimate support to faith. She tried to imagine the world as Mengele must see it, postvision: the stone-cold nothing on the inside of every visible creature, all the heat on the surface, love and hate both reduced to inevitable friction, to clash. It was like living, she imagined, in a condition of perpetual war. Looking into the blank abyss of his world made her sick to her stomach. She willed herself back to sleep.

At class in the morning her students told her that the nurse, Doña Marciana, had seen a luxury automobile—she thought it was a Mercedes—come through Potrerito during the night. It stopped in front of Mengele's house, the motor running quietly. Ña Marciana, who had been out late attending to a snake-bitten child in the next village, watched but saw no one leave the vehicle. Nor did Mengele come out of his shack, as far as she could tell. But first thing in the morning everybody up had watched him take off, running almost, to the little store at the other end of the village. He bought a tin of spiced beef, some eggs, a can of peaches in syrup, paid for them with a new ten-thousand-Guarani note. This was before the fifty-thousand bill had been introduced, and new ten-thousands were rare in Potrerito.

Through the fall and into early winter the same expensive car—more than one person saw it, and it was definitely a Mercedes—came through every two weeks. Always at night and never at the same time. People tried, but no one ever managed to see the driver, or any passenger, descend from the vehicle. Nevertheless, after every visit Mengele had cash to spend on food and the other simple luxuries to be found in the village.

The observable upswing Mengele experienced when the weather cooled and the mysterious luxury automobile began bringing him spending money ended with the visit of the colonels. It was the first time in anyone's memory that a colonel made the trip to Potrerito. The village had nothing to offer: no tribute, no intelligence, no relevance. Mengele was away collecting medicine in the woods the day three tight-lipped men with stars on their shoulders showed up asking questions. No one had anything to say. They wound up at the school, like all visitors, because *la señorita directora* Pilar knew how to handle outsiders. She was not cowed, gave back as good as she got.

She told them what she knew, omitting her visit to Encarnación and the dentist who had removed a poison tooth. "Who is he?" she asked the one who seemed to be in charge. He was a reserved man with heavy features: deep, sagging pouches below his eyes, a fleshy upper lip that wanted to seal his mouth, and deep, ugly pockmarks across his cheeks, tracks left from a disease that didn't quite kill him. He accepted the hollow cow horn filled with *yerba mate*, sucked meditatively on the metal straw as though he hadn't had a drink of *terere* in a long time. But he proved what Pilar knew, that if they knew anything about Potrerito's Mengele they weren't going to give it away to a person of as little consequence as she.

Mengele was late coming out of the woods that evening. When he finally surfaced, moving in a slow lope like some gaunt, misplaced animal, the children of Potrerito were waiting to give him the news they knew he must dread. And from his reaction, he did. He reached for and grabbed a handy boy of eight, all elbows and ankles, shook him by the neck while the others looked on, out of reach. "Who were they?" he demanded. In his state of high emotion his Guarani became dysfunctional, and he badgered the boy in Spanish with a stiff German accent.

"Mengele hunters," one of the children told him.

The old man let his victim go, turned to face his accusers. "What did you say?" he barked harshly at them.

"Mengele hunters, that's who they are," they chanted at him, having understood it was what he least wanted to hear. "Mengele hunters," they taunted him. "They came to get Mengele."

Pilar was not there to see it, but she believed the account she heard, that he dropped his basket of natural medicines, made a series of ineffectual charges at the kids who ringed him, cursed them in German, and stomped away to his house.

The next morning he didn't come out, refused to open the door to the woman whose turn it was to bring him breakfast. His Guarani was back, and it was foul. She left the covered plate on the threshold and went away holding her breath. In the afternoon Pilar knocked persistently until he opened up growling.

The change shocked her. The man was disintegrating, decaying at high speed. His hair dried into brittle sticks that stuck out every which way on his head. Pallor blanched his face, on which the skin had begun to shrink; the outlines of his cheekbones forced her to visualize the grinning skull he would become. It was cool, but greasy lines of sweat ran the length of his body. His arms hung listlessly at his sides, but his hands twisted incessantly.

"You're a very sick man," she told him. "If you won't take a priest then accept a doctor."

"I am a doctor."

She was cruel, she was curious. "Do you believe in God?" she asked him.

The question made him laugh. He nodded furiously. "God is the face of our need," he told her, "and he is prolific: He has created as many Hells as there are human minds to conceive them."

"What did you say to the Polish priest that time?"

The question, she could tell, offended him, or was it her temerity in assuming that she could understand? Nevertheless he answered her. "A mouse cannot confess a lion. Each species has its own language, and only like can talk to like. All the rest is just interspecies babbling."

"Are you who they say you are?"

He called her something like *village idiot* in Guarani, tottered away back into his shack, and she left well enough alone.

They were fascinated by the spectacle of his decline, but the villagers of Potrerito were tired of taking his abuse, and Pilar could not convince them to go on with their mealtime rotation. So she took over the task herself, fed him and watched for three days as he suffered on his back in his bed inside the shack, which was damp, cold, and unhealthy through the short days of June winter. It's not too late to be sorry, she told him periodically, because it was her duty and because his response thrilled her. The venom of a hundred snakes poured from his mouth. She was cursed in many languages: Guarani, Spanish, German, and others she did not recognize.

But he was sinking steadily. By the third day he had lost the strength to rise on his elbows and rant. Chunks of his yellow-white hair were falling out, and it tired him to keep his eyes open. She bent her head close to his ear, smelled the garlic on his breath, listened carefully as he struggled to formulate what was important to him. "Integrity," he told her. "I thought it was to be found in consistency, in carrying things to their inevitable conclusion. In not being afraid of consequences."

"And it wasn't?" Unconsciously she, too, was whispering, leaning still closer to him.

Outside, a horse chomped grass noisily near the bedside wall. The noise was inane, maddening, too close to their conversation. She had never visited such a place before.

"It wasn't? Then where is integrity?" she pushed him, not sure what her question meant or why she asked it. She waited, afraid he had gone to sleep, or passed away.

He hadn't. After a few moments he answered with restrained conviction. "In the purity, the clarity of your vision. But only in the moment. When you begin to act on vision you are already polluting it."

"I don't understand."

His laugh was too weak to scald, but she felt the heat of his derision faintly, faintly. "Explain yourself," she insisted. She wanted to shake him but knew he could bear no serious pressure just then.

He relented, or else he was only humoring himself again. "There is a moment," he told her, "between the vision and what you make of it, how you translate it into action, or an idea, when the power is perfect, it's undiluted. That moment is what one lives for. It's the place where pleasure begins. Tragedy happens when one realizes he cannot live in that terrible place, he cannot stay close to such perfect pleasure. All the rest, everything that comes afterward, is a compromise, and therefore to be despised."

"Not tragedy," she said, hoping to provoke him into continuing, but he was unable or unwilling to say more. She spoonfed him some soup, but his swallowing reflex was misfiring, and the soup dribbled from the side of his mouth like more ugly secrets spilling out. She thought she should send a boy on horseback for the priest in the *pueblo*, but before she could bring herself to decide, on the afternoon of the third day an airplane appeared in the sky over Potrerito.

It was a small craft, twin engine, and the motor noise was oddly animallike. No airplane had ever flown over the village. People stood in front of their doors, in the sandy dirt road, in their cotton fields looking up. The plane made three passes the length, more or less, of the village. Then it turned on its side as if to perform a stunt of some sort, looped back low one last time, came close to grazing Mengele's thatched roof. It sputtered for a moment, the engine almost stalled. But the pilot recovered and the airplane disappeared south, toward Encarnación following the unpaved *ruta*.

Everyone in the neighborhood was there to verify the end of the story, which was not a story but indisputable truth. Before the sound of the aircraft engine died in the distance Mengele had risen from his sickbed, come outside. In his hands he held the big blue book. He was raving in German, it had to be German. He lifted the book toward the sky once, twice, several times, screamed in a fever of rage at anyone and everyone who stood watching, then fell to the ground. They helped him back to his bed, and in the middle of that night he died.

They found him under the bed in a muddy puddle that had formed when it rained and never dried out. His body was folded into the shape babies assumed in the womb; there was something childlike about the corpse, its attitude in death. Pilar did not help to lay him out for burial, so she did not see with her own eyes the daisy chain of swastikas tattooed on his abdomen. The blue leather book, which people called the magic book, was gone. No one ever found it, and people believed each other when they said they hadn't seen it.

They buried him in the cemetery they shared with the next village over, and maybe it would have ended there, a story to be cultivated in the retelling, retooling, rediscovering. But before a week had passed someone came and dug up the body, hauled it away at night leaving the grave gaping empty. A vehicle had been heard, an engine idling. Pilar suspected the Polish priest. The Nazis had killed uncounted Poles, and he must have had connections with people back at home who dealt with matters like this one.

After a lifetime there were still things she recognized but did not understand, such as why the removal of Mengele's bones freed the villagers of Potrerito to do what they did.

She left her early supper uneaten at the tail end of the short day, strolled through the village toward the knotted crowd. They had already doused the shack with gasoline. They were worked up, drinking cane whiskey, and consequently incoherent. When they saw her they shut up, and the one with the torch lifted let it drop, smoking, onto the wet grass. It smoldered.

This was the darkness she knew. With just a little light—in her hand, in her head—she had sway over them, as always, and authority. They respected something in her they could not have named.

"Mengele!" someone yelled in her direction, sideways so as not to catch her directly with the force of his feeling. "This is Mengele's house."

They waited. They were good at waiting, good at giving way. Pilar herself was frozen, temporarily. The sun got hung up on the arms of the western trees, where it split open over the woods dripping color that was quickly sponged up by the lowering dark. The postsunset wind stood up and started running. This was the darkness she knew, the darkness whose hegemony she contested.

She was not like herself. It was the stuff of stories, just as true. Besides, there were witnesses, more than the most unlikely story required. They watched her pick up the smoldering torch, shake it in the air until it burst again into flame, and advance on the house. It went up fast. It was Mengele's house. There was nothing inside.

how birds
communicate

This has to be done from the outside. If I went inside, and you followed me, we'd both be lost, possibly forever. You'll trust me on this, but first I want to give you a few unassailable facts. When I say unassailable, I mean objective. Being objective is what a person does to stay on the outside. That's the theory. Anyway, here are the facts:

1. My father, who was tortured and then disappeared by government goons during the Stroessner dictatorship in Paraguay, named me Lenín. He chose to do this at a time when literature and beards were both considered prima facie evidence of the worldwide communist conspiracy at work in our country.

2. At one point during one of the torture sessions, the goons placed a telephone call to my mother and allowed her to listen to my father's screams of pain. The experience of listening brought on

a mental breakdown in my mother. She did not recover. She chose, rather, to go inside.

3. The arrest, torture, and disappearance of my father were ordered by a very fat man named Pastor Coronel, one of the dictator Stroessner's most faithful and efficient supporters. Government documents substantiate this. After Stroessner fell from power, Pastor Coronel was charged with many heinous crimes, including several related to my father. Because our legal system is dysfunctional, these charges have not been resolved by trial. Pastor Coronel remains in preventive detention.

4. Pastor Coronel's health is poor.

5. Pastor Coronel's name is a disturbing oxymoron.

Strictly speaking, we should strike statement number four from my list of facts. (I say *we* because I want to get close to you. You are where I want to be, i.e., on the outside.) My information regarding Coronel's health was secondhand. It came from newspaper accounts suggesting that he was ill in body and soul. It was evident, however, that although he had lost some weight his obesity was a tremendous drag on the man. It was a recent photograph and article in *Noticias*, actually, that broke a certain impasse for me. The photo, or more accurately my reaction to it, led me to act. The reaction was sympathy. There ought to be a hell for persons who feel it.

I try not to read the papers. When I do, I focus on the economic news. I work for a small think tank that studies economic phenomena and applies the results to indices you might broadly label as quality-of-life issues. The Centro de Luz got its start with international funding back during the dictatorship, when it was impossible to conduct research in the universities. Luz survived because foreign embassies lobbied with the regime to keep it open, although we were continually harassed by thugs in uniforms and lackeys armed with official paperwork.

Luz was the logical choice of employment for the son of a man murdered for his political convictions. My father's convictions were simple: He insisted on people's right to express an opinion. If enough people shared a particular opinion—for instance, that the distribution of land and wealth in a given subtropical country with a history of de facto government was inequitable—then serious consideration ought to be given to changing that distribution. When he was murdered I was twenty-three. I inherited his convictions, which naturally diluted over time into beliefs.

My father was a visionary. He dreamt and described a city of justice. My task was less grandiose. I was one of many architects in a firm whose prosaic contract was to build such a city, brick by humble brick.

I cut out the picture from *Noticias* and hung it in the rim of the bathroom mirror. I studied it as I shaved, after I showered, while I dressed. In the photo, Pastor Coronel sits on the edge of his bed in pajamas and slippers, one hand up to shield his face from the photographer's prying eye. The hospital bed is mussed, the striped sheets tangled. Even in the grainy picture his great bulk exudes discomfort; it leaks like sweat from the man's pores.

Across from the patient-prisoner sits an outlandish man in a tight white suit. He is as fat as Coronel himself. A garish tie rides becalmed on his vast belly. He has turned mid-gesture to look at the photographer, and his jowly face in square black glasses shows surprise, irritation, and that unmistakable lust for publicity one sees in so many faces these days. His outrage is phony. He loves being photographed ministering to the notorious anticommunist.

The accompanying article describes Coronel's interlocutor as a forensic psychiatrist. I knew from friends that as a young man he was a poet with exuberant socialist ideals, and that he failed at medical school. He was himself arrested and imprisoned. Behind bars he underwent an ideological conversion that straightened his twisted vision, returning to the streets a virulent supporter of President Alfredo Stroessner, who gave him work. The journalist quoted him as saying that if Pastor Coronel continued the way he was going, the former chief of the Department of Investigations of the

Asunción Police would kill himself. He suffered from an over-whelming combination of physical and mental maladies, including bulimia, a reluctance to get out of bed, and a severe persecution complex.

I folded the photograph and tucked it into my wallet. Down-stairs, my mother had the *mate* ready. I'm a compulsive early riser, subject to anxiety if I don't see the sun rise, as though I've missed something I need. For years Mother and I have enjoyed a little morning ritual. For forty minutes we sit in the back patio and she serves me hot *mate*, maintaining the water in the kettle just below the boiling point on a gas ring.

"Two woodpeckers," she said, handing me the gourd with the strong, bitter tea. "They said there was a terrible storm off the coast of Chile. A banana boat went down with all hands. An albatross saw it sink."

I sat next to her and sucked on the silver straw. The dark had not quite lifted. I couldn't make out the woodpeckers, but Mother's eyesight was always acute. Our house sits in the middle of a block-long street of irregular cobbles in Villa Laureles. The house is quite small but attractive to the eye. It once appeared on a postcard. My father was the one who converted the back patio into a garden. It has been a pleasant oasis, with corn and tomato and pepper and bean plants, flowers and ornamental shrubs. Around the cultivated perimeter orange and grapefruit trees alternate in a protective row.

And birds. Since my father died, I should say. While he was alive we had birds, of course. What city garden doesn't draw them? But when my mother went into her decline, it was as though they smelled it, and we were inundated. Birds of every description, birds not normally found in the city, common birds and uncommon birds, brilliant and dull birds, long-tailed and short. We had to buy a book to identify them. They didn't stay long, and sometimes it was one lone representative of a species that showed up for an hour and left again. But they came, they kept coming, they have never stopped coming.

My older brother Derlis believes that the birds began to come because the garden had reached a certain level of mature profusion, and they were attracted to the varied bounty it offered. According to Derlis, the birds have nothing to do with my father's being taken away and my mother's reaction to the loss. Derlis is a physician, a surgeon, with a comfortable private practice and a summer apartment on the beach in Punta del Este. He is highly skilled at his job. My complaint about him is the assumption he makes that since he can deal with the mysteries of the body, he somehow understands the other mysteries that people inhabit.

Apart from the pleasure intrinsic to observing such flitting variety, the birds were a godsend for Mother. She began gradually to communicate with them. Derlis and I have gone round and round on this. He considers I am being willful in my description of what happens out there in the garden. Anyone who would play with the idea of interspecies communication he views as tending toward instability, a condition my brother Derlis abhors. If you incline to his side, I'd only point out the curious (but unassailable) fact that while my father lived in the house we had an ordinary urban allotment of birds—a jay here, a sparrow there—while afterward they came in herds.

Over the years the birds have meant a great deal to Mother. I believe she could not live without them. A few years ago when my marriage was tottering, we sent her to live with each of my sisters and brothers in turn. The idea was to give my wife and me some privacy to work things out. My siblings were all willing to take her in, but the most Mother lasted was two weeks with my youngest sister. Although she claimed she was restless without me, I believe it was the birds she really missed. (After tottering, my marriage crashed, but for reasons that have nothing to do with Pastor Coronel. My wife took our children to Buenos Aires, where she married a plastic surgeon whose only defect, to my knowledge, was a disparaging way he had of raising his eyebrows when my name was mentioned in the presence of the kids. I never saw him do it, of course, but it has been described to me by people I trust.)

As the sun came up over Asunción and the traffic stirred, we drank our *mate* and watched a pair of woodpeckers investigate the trunk of a grapefruit tree. A yellow-and-black *pitogüe* foraged below them in the corn. And my mother narrated a story in several voices that I assumed she picked up from the birds. It was the animal equivalent of a soap opera, too theatrical for my taste. I distrust emotion when it's noisy. It took place on the Argentine pampa and included foxes and deer and cow ponies and red hawks, as far as I could make out. Mother never explained her stories. I was her only audience, and I was incidental.

As I listened passively and the *mate* woke me up and I felt the summer heat of February assert its prerogative on the humid air, an idea formed in me. It began as an idle fantasy, but in the course of the day at Luz it acquired a shape, a body, and finally a life of its own. I tacked the photo of Pastor Coronel and the forensic psychiatrist on the bulletin board on my office wall. It disappointed me that no one noticed or commented on it. Perhaps my colleagues assumed out of delicacy that reference to it would be painful. By midmorning I shut the door, stopped working, and stared into the picture with my hands folded on the desktop.

The absurd photograph that captured a moment in the history of injustice in our country was not the first of its kind, just the most provoking. In their blunt, battering way trying to make democracy work, journalists periodically stole their way into wherever Coronel was being held, snapped him in his bed of pain, and appended to the picture an article describing the snail's pace at which the legal system was moving toward justice.

Each time I saw one of those articles, I was overcome with a strange sensation for which I have no more accurate word than sympathy. I imagined what it must be to move in one's life from a torturer with unlimited scope of action, reporting directly to the President, who trusted him for reasons no outsider would ever know, to a prisoner in a timeless limbo of pain and uncertainty. He knew he was reviled, and that the dictatorship was gone for good, and that the most he could look forward to was a jail sentence that would last longer than he did. Gone forever the pleasures of power and the unchecked ability to hurt people. Gone all the secret satisfactions: the terrified, pliant young girls whose mothers thrust them forward as payment in kind for consumer goods. The camaraderie of men who ruled. The certainty, in which lurked a strangely sexual impulse, that when common citizens recognized one's official automobile on the street, they quailed, or prayed, and then hid their relief when it passed them by.

It was almost as if I were able to get inside the ugly, obese body of the torturer and experience what he felt, what he suffered. I could rub my palm across the textured surface of his nightmares. All this for the man who had my father killed. You can imagine how I felt. Whenever it happened, a tremendous self-loathing engulfed me, paralyzed me, blinded me. I could not look at myself in the mirror. It was all I could do to stay inside my body as it walked in the street, or drove my car, or sat in the morning to drink *mate* and listen to my mother's amazing stories. It was my own dirty secret, and there was no one in whom I could confide it for the simple relief of letting it out. I could say more but prefer not to, hoping you will respect the reticence.

The only way out, it occurred to me as I sat in my office listening to the computer's conspiratorial whisper, was to kill Pastor Coronel. Since his health had deteriorated he had been moved to the Adventist Hospital, where security was lax, as the photographer from *Noticias* had proven. I could use the same ploy: borrow a camera and sneak or bribe my way in. Or I could pretend to be a doctor. Paraguayans seldom challenged a person who appeared to know what he was about; that was one more residue of the authoritarian manner in which the place had been governed for so long. But I opted for neither of those. Instead I became a janitor, probably because the challenge of pulling off the character appealed to me. A dry run was advisable.

That same day I found myself pushing a broom down a hall in

the Adventist Hospital dressed the way any other janitor dressed, aping the resignation of body with which I had observed them go about their duties, as if in their heart of hearts they suspected that if there were a Heaven, and they made it that far, they would wind up pushing a broom across the celestial floor because of an uncorrectable flaw in the nature of things. In my pocket I carried a hunk of smooth wood in place of the pistol I was going to need. There was only one tense moment, when a woman I knew from the Foreign Ministry happened down the hall. But I hung my head and kept sweeping, and she blew by me on a wind of purpose quite certain she had nothing to say to a custodian like me.

As much as practicing the janitor act itself I needed to locate Pastor Coronel's room without giving myself away, and as it turned out I stumbled across it quite by chance. I had acquired a little squeaky-wheeled cart piled high with the tools of my new trade and was roaming the halls randomly when a door opened, a nurse with a clipboard exited, and I saw the giant belly of the man who had killed my father rise and fall regularly as he lay sleeping on his back. For the moment, at least, there was no police guard. In a country in which the principal henchmen of the dictator still strolled the streets freely, living off the investments they made during the fat times, perhaps it was thought that the former head of *Investigaciones* was safe as he was.

At any rate I had my first glimpse of Coronel in the flesh, albeit asleep. The sight of him that way—flat on his back in a bed too small to contain him, his asthmatic breathing like a kind of nonverbal stutter—brought on a flood of sympathy. I fingered the block of wood in my pocket for a moment, turned and rolled my cart away, and I was gone.

At home, Mother was elated by a visitation: Seventeen hummingbirds had descended on the garden in a cloud of nervous color. They spent the afternoon among the flowering shrubs like so many finicky epicures delighted to have stumbled across a five-star restaurant in a sleepy town in the south of France. I could scarcely pay attention to Mother, the self-loathing had risen to such a pitch inside me. I was sick to my stomach, and cold sweats broke out on my body, which felt weak and unnaturally sensitive.

"There are still wildcats in the jungle," my mother told me. She was making me a sandwich in the kitchen, and I felt pleased to see her so animated, so evidently satisfied with her life and circumstances and my sonly love. "But not so many as there used to be."

"People have no notion of what they do when they shoot one," I said.

She shook her head and grinned. Her delight in knowing something I didn't know hurt me. "That's not the problem, Lenín. They told me this afternoon what the real problem is. If anyone, bird or beast or human, dares to count them all and then say the number out loud, the cats will die. Every last one of them. Don't you think that would be a shame, *mi hijo?*"

I agreed it would be a shame. I took my cheese sandwich, along with some baked *chipitas* and a glass of cold water. I despised myself. When I had eaten and my mother left the room, I tore the photograph from *Noticias* into a dozen pieces. And I made up my mind.

The next morning I called in sick and went downtown, where it was only too easy to purchase a Remingon pistol and some ammunition. The Korean merchant who sold me the gun did not ask to see any identification. He tried instead to interest me in a contraband stereo system, which he had in great quantity in stacks around the shop. I knew I should take the time to familiarize myself with the weapon before I used it to kill someone, but I was quite sure that not unless and until Pastor Coronel was dead by my hand would I be rid of the clammy feeling of self-disgust that hung on me like a skin. I was impatient not to do it but for it to be over. Plus it would be dangerous to climb down from the wave of momentum that was carrying me along.

So it all happened fast, just like the movies. There I was in the men's lavatory at the hospital dressing myself in the custodian's uniform, loading my new gun, retrieving what looked like the same squeaky-wheeled cart from a dark closet that smelled like mothballs and soap. To steady my nerves I wheeled the cart around the halls aimlessly for a while, happy that no one paid the least attention to me. I could have stayed inside that moment of sealed suspension forever.

But I didn't, of course. Here I was, or someone who resembled me except that he was more purposeful, opening the door to the sick man's room. Coronel was awake, as he should be. The persecution complex had caused the equivalent of supersensitive miniature antennae to grow on his body like invisible fur. Those antennae told him instantly that I was not the normal custodian, and that I might hurt him. He heaved himself up into a sitting position, which effort caused him to lose the little breath he had, and he stared at me as though keen to know the particulars of the grudge I bore him.

I pulled the pistol from the pocket of my jacket. It had the heft of the hunk of wood I had used during the dry run. I released the safety, pointed the weapon at his guilty heart, and steadied my aim with my free hand. The torturer's mouth opened slowly in a round O of supplication and terror. He raised his arms slowly into the position of surrender. Urine leaked in a slow stream from his pajama pants, then onto the floor. By the time I squeezed the trigger, unfortunately, there was someone behind me. A plainclothes policeman, I think, although my memory is patchy and inclined to play tricks when I reconstruct all this. I also remember an intern in a white smock and wire-rimmed glasses, and someone burly who smelled like tobacco and may have been a real janitor.

I'm not sure which one of the three got to me first. Whoever it was he spoiled my aim so that the bullet caught Coronel in the shoulder, quite high. Flesh and blood splatted in a satisfying way, and the torturer roared in pain that came out as outrage. Someone knocked me to the ground, and I lost the gun. But when I got to my feet there he was sitting on the bed, bleeding and laughing. He pointed his finger at me and shot.

"Gotcha," he said, and I understood perfectly that he had.

★ ★ ★

The cell they locked me inside was blessedly quiet. There were official things to be done, I gathered, before I was remanded to the common penitentiary known popularly as the Tacumbu Hilton. It was a perfect place not to think but to meditate in a way that called upon powers of imagination I hadn't known I possessed. With your forbearance, I prefer not to go into detail. I thought, as you might expect, about my father. I thought about Pastor Coronel, and President Alfredo Stroessner in exile in Brazil, and some of the other victims of the regime about whom I had read over the years. I thought about being on the inside, how different it was from being on the outside, as though there really were two distinct worlds, and the great cunning mystery to be understood was the way the intersection points were hidden, so that one never knew when he might step out of one into the other. I thought about Pastor Coronel pointing his finger at me and shooting. However ugly the knowledge, it pained me to learn something from him.

At one point a noisy swarm of newspaper people was allowed inside to take my picture. I had nothing to say in response to their questions, which were predictable and blind-eyed, just what one would expect from people on the outside without a clue about the inside. Happily for me, friends and lawyers arranged to have me released on their recognizance. There was a swelling up of popular sympathy for me, since my intended victim was a man who deserved whatever he ultimately got. The media fanned the flame, printing stories about my father and his vision of the just city. People who had lost loved ones to the goons organized a vigil in front of the court building, and something quiet about their conviction threatened people in the government, who thought to defuse the tension and earn some easy credit at the same time by letting me out of prison. I was escorted home not like a hero who had achieved something, or tried to achieve something, but like a man who had suffered a recent bereavement and needed gentling.

My mother knew all about what had happened, she told me when they left us to ourselves. She hadn't worried when I failed to come home from work on time. A rare visitor had explained it all to her. It was her first sighting of a short-billed canastero. Proudly she showed me the picture in our well-thumbed bird book. She had printed a careful *X* next to the paragraph describing the bird. *X* meant she made the first sighting; my mark was a Z.

"What did it tell you, Mother?"

"Let's drink some *mate*," she suggested.

It was early. The day was going to be a scorcher. But *mate* sounded good. I felt more at peace than I had for a long time. The anxiety was gone. So was the self-loathing. They drained out of me while I sat in the cell waiting to be charged with attempted murder. In their place was nothing, which was extremely buoyant, like a raft or a cushion.

Mother waited until the water was hot on the gas ring and she had passed me the gourd full of tea before she answered my question.

"It had to do with your father, didn't it," she said hesitantly.

I was amazed. Not twice in a year did she bring up his name. "It did."

"Your sister Julia tried to trick me with some cock-and-bull story about your running into a friend from school who invited you out to his ranch in the Chaco."

"Julia meant well, Mother."

"But I knew better."

"What did you know?"

"I knew . . ." She was crying. "I knew the number."

"What number?"

"How many wildcats are left in Paraguay."

That made sense. I nodded, and she excused herself. She wanted to do some tidying up around the house, after all the commotion of visitors. She may not have known what she was doing—I'm reasonably certain that she didn't—but I did. She was tempting me to go where she had gone. Inside. I won't go.

I sat by myself drinking *mate* until the strength of the *yerba* was spent. The serenity I felt was anything but lassitude. It was too clean for that, too round. I watched a white-tipped dove settle in an orange tree, the branch on which it lit swaying slightly with the bird's weight. The question in my mind was where a person wanted to live his life: outside or in. I made my choice years ago. I will stay outside. With you. I've been inside. It's more like a cell than a cage. Not that it's always easy to know what's best. But the serenity helped. When the dove opened its small bill to speak I stopped my ears.

the rape of reason

The rape of reason was tantamount, for Don Martín del Valle, to the snuffing out of civilization. The violation occurred over time, in a series of events the connections among which were not always transparent, even after he began watching for them. It began with the inexplicable suicide of a Great Andean hummingbird. One moment working its wings in the crystalline *paceño* air above his white roses, the next, the elegant green creature hurled itself against the glass of his kitchen window and fell dead in a bush. Leaving his coffee, Martín went outside and picked up the corpse. He cupped it in his hand. Stilled, the wings were preposterous: unlikely appendages to a body so fragile it felt, in his dry palms, like a leaf. He buried the bird in the rich dirt of his roses with a trowel and went back inside to hear himself excoriated on the radio.

Not himself, exactly, or not that anyone knew. The source of contention was his column in *El Diario*. Striving for irony back in 1970 when he began writing, he had titled his offering "In the Shadow of the Martyr's Bones." The martyr's bones was a tree that required constant nourishment, long years, and much luck to flourish. When it finally grew to a size large enough to shelter, its thin conical leaves cast precious little shade, and the pale gray twigs and branches, like stubby bones, that gave the tree its name could cause it to appear, in just the right light, almost insubstantial, the idea of a tree rather than the thing itself.

The voice on the radio fulminating against the cowardly author of the column belonged to the leader of one of the unions, now so diminished in strength that their threats to paralyze and remake Bolivia were as hollow as their rhetoric. Nevertheless, strident and uncontaminated by doubt, the voice repeated a charge that had first surfaced in the early seventies: There was no Forastero Azúl, the pen name that had occurred to Martín when Serapio insisted the column be signed. In the nineties the Blue Stranger sounded as ridiculous as it was whimsical, but stubbornness and tradition glued him fast to the name. The old theory held that the Forastero Azúl was not a man but a fictional mouthpiece for the voices of reaction, who were too cowardly to own up to their dirty hunger for the bad old days when a gentleman of property could freely exercise his God-given right to abuse the indigenous population, the semiserfs whose labor kept him wealthy and pampered. *El Diario* was a notoriously reactionary newspaper and therefore more than capable of foisting that rhetorical fraud on the reading public of La Paz.

How could one remake a nation that had not quite been made in the first place? Or not yet. The lack of precision in the union man's language set Martín's teeth on edge. What they had accomplished with their drivel and their pugilist's ideology and their crude, blind zeal was the abasement of the word, which, one time long ago having been made flesh, now stood tragically separate from the body to which it was mystically linked, or ought to be. Words, in the Bolivia in which Martín del Valle endured his long interior exile, were stones for assaulting an opponent.

He telephoned Serapio at the paper. "I've made a decision," he told his friend and editor.

"Not to listen to the radio?"

Martín pictured him at his desk: cold coffee and slow, permanent cigarettes, peering through his bifocal lenses at the computer screen as though if he looked carefully enough it would reveal in outline the base political treachery he feared was behind the most innocuous articles. His hard, massive belly was shoved tight against the edge of his desk. Serapio had accomplished what was generally thought impossible in La Paz, which was in essential respects a small town. In all those years, all those three-times-a-week columns, he had kept a secret. No one in Bolivia had tumbled to the true identity of the Forastero Azúl.

"I'm going to drop the pseudonym. I wish you to attach my signature to the column, beginning today."

"You know I'm not going to do that, Don Martín. You've offended too many people to run that risk. What brought this on? Your skin has never been this thin before."

The inexplicable death of a hummingbird, Martín did not risk telling him. Serapio was just enough younger than he that he might be tempted to suspect senility. Degradation of the man and his capacity to reason was a possibility not to be given scope. "Do it, please," he instructed the editor.

"I'll call you back before we go to press. That will give you time to reconsider."

"I won't."

In the unlit hallway of the house he inherited from his dispossessed parents, Martín cradled the old-fashioned black telephone receiver and began to laugh. Not hysterically, but neither was he in control, really, of the strange assortment of sounds—bass boomings and treble tweets and breathy barks—that came up and out of him.

He was not a person who laughed, not like that anyway, like a circus clown burlesquing his own absurd comic style. Martín del Valle was the king of reason, uncrowned and uncontested in his right to rule his invisible, profitless domain. Such laughter was a deformation.

Eventually it subsided, and he went into the living room to read. But before he picked up the Greek grammar that lay open on one of the meter-high stacks of compacted knowledge that tracked, albeit irregularly, the history of his intellectual curiosity, he was transfigured. No; more accurate to say that he was seduced by the transfiguration of the proximate world that occurred as he stepped into the sunlight there. The house in Miraflores had been built to accommodate a view of Mount Ilimani that dominated the city, as if the designer had held up the enormous plate-glass window and ordered them to construct a residence around it. The light of La Paz, demonstrably different from the light of any other city in the world—it had to do with the filtering of the air, a mysterious natural process not yet fully understood by scientists—flooded through the glass and hallowed the hundreds of books, the piles of magazines and journals and newspapers from Paris and Buenos Aires and New York, the tired upholstered furniture suitable for a sedentary scholar, the reading lamps placed strategically by all his favorite nooks, the family pictures on the papered walls. This, he understood, was the instant toward which the universe had been so patiently evolving all those billions of unhuman years. Right here, in the room in which he had lived his life.

For the first time in memory he felt lonely, a sensation like a giddy longing for something that smelled narcotically sweet but had no face, no discernible shape, no name. A sense of having been abandoned threatened to bring on tears or, even worse, that uncontrolled laughter again. He had not chosen this solitude; it was forced on him. In 1952, when the revoluntary MNR government appropriated the del Valle mines and *haciendas* and made bitter pilgrims of his parents, Martín was twenty-seven and irresponsibly earnest. His doctorate in medieval European history from the University of

Chicago had not prepared him adequately for the chaos and carnage he came home just in time to witness. In Miraflores, the abolishment of flogging was celebrated by the public flogging of a *criollo* landowner arrogant enough to spit at the feet of Indians he was accustomed to command. Unadaptable, the man died. Less dramatic and more pliable, Martín's parents took what was portable and bought a house in rural Connecticut. They had been prudent enough to invest abroad, in what his father Don Porfirio called the civilized world, so they were not afforded the moral luxury of becoming destitute. As victims went, they were more than comfortable. They coped, they carped. They refused to understand.

Martín's three sisters went with them and found, in quick succession, North American husbands who spoke no Spanish and whose imaginations and energies were oriented to making money. They did not refuse to understand the revolution in the wilds of the Andes, they simply didn't think about it.

Come! came insistent messages from Connecticut, and New York, and Northern California. For several years. But Martín stayed put in Bolivia, and eventually his family wrote him off as a stubborn eccentric whose native weakness of character had been unfortunately magnified by prolonged graduate study in the United States. He made sure to visit the Colossus of the North every two years, in December, where he dutifully recounted around the Christmas dinner table how bad things were in Bolivia, learning to enjoy and even to induce the ritualistic expressions of horror his stories provoked:

. . . every time the President goes into a meeting with the union the presses start printing money, and the worst of it is the union people know there's nothing to stand behind the paper. They're willing to drive inflation up into the clouds so long as they can go back to their *bases* and report a pay raise . . . ¡*que increíble!*

. . . every year at the beginning of the semester I take my own unofficial little poll, out of curiosity, you know, and every semester at least one student walks through my door willing to admit he's never read a book in his life, not a single book . . . *¡que vergüenza!*

. . . they're victims, really, that's the sad part. Overnight the organizers nailed up wooden crosses to the gates in front of the university and then bound half a dozen out-of-work miners to them. Yes, men and women both. In the morning, with the sun coming up over the canyon, the sight of symbolically crucified miners hanging there was enough to take a person's breath away. . . *¡que barbaridad!*

Nevertheless he was luckier than many. Back when it could have been at risk, the house in Miraflores wasn't noticed or appropriated, perhaps because it was a modest affair, a middle-class dwelling his father had built on a whim for the view of the talismanic, domineering mountain, and as an investment. It was impossible, in Martín's circumstances, to avoid developing a crusade, but he took pains that his own be—he thought at the time—realistic. He went into the university to teach history, a laudable pursuit in its own regard. But what he really wanted to achieve was more ambitious. He sought to inculcate, in students who resisted it blindly, the use of reason. He would play his part, however modest, in the education of a generation who would shine the light of reason and logic and clarified thought onto the murky plain of politics, and the quality of Bolivian life would rise in proportion to the intensity of their light.

It didn't work. He lasted until 1968, a year when it seemed possible to almost anyone that the holy world revolution was going to be accomplished by the simple force of passion, without the need of reason. In a secret session of the university council to which he was not invited he was accused of being an imperialist propagandist, a reactionary brake on the wheel of progress, which turned ineluctably, and they let him go. *Come!* his parents and his sisters pleaded when they learned he had been fired. You've done enough to salve the conscience of the most scrupulous saint in the history of the planet's injustices. But he did not come. Couldn't, probably. What he did, instead, was survive.

The transfiguration of his living room faded with the light, which went rapidly as if to remind Martín he was seventy years old and had better pay strict attention to what was offered in the way of vision, which went, if you let it, beyond mere spectacle. For dinner he ate a roll with butter and drank a mugful of chamomile tea. When Serapio called to convince him not to confess ownership of his problematic column he told him, "*Alea jacta est*," and went to sleep lulled by the austere fatalism of the famous phrase, and a sense of unexpected relief that was linked dimly with the unaccountable outburst of laughing he had suffered that afternoon.

He had lost interest in his dreams years ago when they seemed, as he dredged them up, to reduce to a mishmash of private trash, the flotsam and jetsam tossed by his sly, unconscious self onto the surface of the sea of sleep, which was one more useful name for oblivion. But the vivid, evocative dream he experienced that night would not allow itself to be ignored. In it he became a fearsome but attractive creature, part bird, part beast, part finely pitched human intelligence. Flying across mountains that resembled the Andes in their sublime and sere indifference, he distinctly felt the air cool on his skin, his feathers, on his horny face. When he swooped the place he landed was female, and the sex that happened intoxicated him, body and brain and birdlike imagination. The loss he felt on waking was strong enough to brand the details of the dream in his memory.

The telephone before coffee was Serapio.

"You sound pretty good for a dead man."

"No riddles, please. It's too early."

"Look at *Presencia*. The obituaries."

The broken-shoe'd, under-educated *canillita* on the street who sold the gray scholar his morning paper had no idea he was taking money from the hand of a dead man. The thought gave Martín a brief, disturbing thrill that had to do with anonymity and witness. At any rate the dream—most likely the sex in it—had invigorated him, and back home with the comfort of strong coffee he read his obituary in *Presencia* with the attitude of a man strong enough to see his fate and bear it.

Martín del Valle, of La Paz: taken to his rest unexpectedly by complications brought on by a lifetime of reactionary propagandizing. He is survived by several sisters as reactionary as he, currently resident in the United States of North America, where they continue to live off the ill-gotten gains of their parents, oligarchs displaced by the events of 1952. Characterized by his unremitting hostility to the Bolivian people, del Valle was unable to reconcile himself to their legitimate aspirations and demands, expending considerable energy in a futile effort to overturn their progress toward justice and equity. In arch-conservative spheres his loss will be mourned.

It was not as poorly written as he had expected. Perhaps he had a literate enemy. He reached for the phone to call Serapio but set it down without dialing. Instead he clipped half a dozen white roses leaving the stems long, the way he seemed to remember that she liked them, wrapped them in the obituary section of *Presencia*, and took a taxi to Montserrat.

"This is just like you, Martín, not to show up until you're dead."

Her impassive Aymara butler, if that was what the man was supposed to be, showed him into her study in the big, elegant, colonial house in Sopocachi. Montserrat was only five years younger than he but looked, to Martín's newly appraising eye, a full generation younger, someone with whom he would find nothing in common. Money, he supposed, was the most effective insulator.

"I had an extraordinary dream last night," he told her. "It was about you."

She arched her eyebrows in an unconvincingly sympathetic gesture he realized he had been thinking about for decades, and she let him study her for a few untroubled moments while the maid brought tea on silver service. The marvelous hair was still shining obsidian, undyed, highlighted only slightly with gray as if for contrast. The wide face, an oval of fierce intelligence (like one of those satellite dishes except that what it trapped was people) was pale but suggested vigor rather than pallor. The nervous thin-fingered hands with bumpy knuckles had not learned how to rest, not in all those years. They opened books and riffled pages, unwrapped the roses, tied and untied the white satin bow around a tin of potpourri that sat open on her desk, drummed and probed and discovered. It appeared that Montserrat had as yet undergone no reverses in her experience-laden life powerful enough to shake her vanity with doubt.

He watched her squeeze lemon expertly into her tea. Martín's parents had a silver tea service like that. When he visited his mother made sure she used it.

"'So, the door opens and there with white roses in his hand stands the man I loved, or should have loved. Still slender and upright, still a gentleman of the old school. Only now he is old in fact as well as habit. I will never forgive you for letting me go, Martín."

"You would not have been content without . . . all this," he told her. "Without enough money to allow you to do every last thing you wanted to do."

But she was not about to be misled by facts, or to let him get the upper hand. "You abandoned me for an ideal. You put the education of something you called the Bolivian *pueblo* above any sort of love for me, and that was thoughtless and shabby. I married Julio out of spite. What should I have done? The money helped, of course. Your tea is getting cold."

Martín considered the possibility that he had stayed in Bolivia as much because she was there as for any idea of education in history and logic and the ineffable virtues of reason. Not that they had stayed in touch much. That would have been too painful, at least for him.

"Something seems to be happening to me, Montserrat. I feel as though I'm losing control of my life. I can see it happening but I can't do anything about it. I'm scared."

"It was foolish of you to sign your real name to the column. I had no idea. I read it, of course. I've always read the Forastero Azúl. I should have known, probably, from the quality of the prose that you were behind it. But what you've done is make yourself a target. Now what will that prove?"

"That's not what's bothering me."

"That only goes to prove again what was true way back when you jilted me, which is how little common sense an intelligent man can demonstrate, sometimes."

"In my dream I was flying. I could feel the air rushing over me. I haven't dreamt about flying for years. Maybe I never did."

"You should leave La Paz for a few weeks, Martín. Drop the column and go someplace nice. I had a letter last week from your sister Angelina. She complains you refuse to visit, and she's worried you will turn eccentric living alone and jousting so stubbornly at the windmills of ignorance. Go see Angelina. Her husband's company just went on the stock exchange in New York, which means their money is doubled, or maybe she said tripled. You can help them celebrate their success."

"It's not too late, Montserrat."

"To celebrate? Of course it isn't. Angelina will be delighted."

"I mean for us. I mean for . . . for love."

By the animal alertness with which she looked at him suddenly across the tea table he knew she was fighting an urge to laugh, possibly hysterically, at his proposal. He was making a fool of himself, a seventy-year-old historian and amateur logician, the author of a monograph on a failed uprising of Quechua Indians in the 1890s that had been printed and reprinted in Argentina, in Chile, had been translated into English and used as a text in Latin American studies programs at a respectable number of U.S. universities.

But she did not laugh, she asked a question. "What did you feel when you heard that Julio had died? What was the first thing you thought?"

Her husband had died ten, perhaps twelve years ago. It was not a question Martín would answer, and she knew it.

"I love you, Montserrat. I believe I always have."

"Don't be absurd. You don't know what you're saying. Take my advice—I'm not a person who gives much, so when I do it's worth something—get out of Bolivia, *querido* Martín. La Paz is a small town. It can drive any thinking person crazy. And it really was a mistake to sign your column. If you won't go north, go to Buenos Aires. See a play, have a suit made. Julio's tailor is wonderful, an Asian of some sort. You know how deferential they can pretend to be when they need to. He must still be there. Where would he go? I can give you the address."

"It's not too late," he insisted. It was the first time he could recall acting so willfully in defiance of his own better judgment. He knew she would laugh as soon as he left. He pictured her doubled up, one hand on her stomach, the other on the door handle. The rape of reason was causing him to regress, to become stupid, as though the disease he fought in others had cunningly invaded his own body.

Then what she told him when she showed him to the door was enough to buckle his knees, bring him so close to the earth that he could hear its ponderous, patient breathing, usually inaudible to rational adults. The sound was hypnotic, and Martín was susceptible.

"I waited, you know, *mi querido.*"

"Waited?"

"For you, Don Martín the obtuse. After I married my Julio. I wanted you to be my lover. That would have made everything perfect. I would have had it all, then: everything a woman requires. But you never came for me. Now it's too late. You're old, aren't you, and I'm on the cusp."

Remarkable. In and out. He heard it, the slow breathing of *la madre tierra*. He could not believe what Montserrat had confessed, or if he believed it he could not take it in and make sense of it.

Nevertheless how fortunate he was to hear that breathing. In and out so slowly it was reassuring. Not everyone was so lucky in his life.

In the cobbled street that sloped through one of the more pleasant sections of Sopocachi down toward the Prado and the noisy center of their mountain city, Martín del Valle's face burned with shame at the ridiculous figure he had made before a mature, wealthy woman to whom he had been attracted years and years before when they were both, in their separate ways, beautiful beings. It was though he had been incontinent in her presence, just what you would expect of an excited old man. He walked home planning the next installment of his column.

★ ★ ★

But it wouldn't come. Evidently his muse needed anonymity. Serapio was happy to let the column lapse for a prudent interval, believing that removing the irritant from the offended eye of whomever it was who had run the obituary would reduce the risk of retaliation. As scrupulous as he was tough on himself, Martín admitted to his friend that he felt relieved not to have to write. Not so much because he expected his words to provoke any repercussions; it was, rather, that his mind had unaccountably seized up. It refused to go through its paces, and the few paragraphs he coaxed out were by turns wooden, stilted, or muddy. What he did not describe to the editor of *El Diario* was the impression of liberation he experienced, like a schoolboy playing hooky. His rate of regression worried him deeply.

There were other things on his mind, however, that occupied his attention profitably. For the next several days he dreamed actively, vociferously, dramatically. In many of the dreams he was a hero, though not always strictly human. In others he was something like the willing victim-host of visitations from creatures, persons, beings of all sorts that enacted their fabulous stories on and around and even underneath him. He flew. He made dream love, solved urgent dream problems. Once, he rescued a woman from murky captivity only to find that she was something else entirely, an intelligent creature that walked on four legs and needed intensive reassurance, and her story, which he obtained in bits and pieces as she whispered into his ear, was a tragedy in the strict sense of the word.

He thought about recording the dreams in a notebook but decided against that. Conscious intervention might staunch the flow, and he was quickly becoming drugged by his dreams; he needed what they gave him. An opponent on principle of the siesta, which he considered an excuse to justify low per-capita productivity, he found himself taking frequent catnaps, at almost any hour, surprised and pleased by the ease with which he could slip into sleep and thence into dream. He sat in his living room, Mount Ilimani staring in (he was accustomed to the mountain's baleful countenance intruding like that), spread *Le Monde* on his lap, switched on a reading lamp, and slept. And dreamed.

And loved, or tried to. He could put up with the private embarrassment of so much dreaming and dithering. He could even accept gracefully the maddening block in his production, in his ability to reason, which might be explained by stress and isolation and was in any case temporary. What he could not abide was the fool he kept making of himself with Montserrat.

He called her, he went to see her. He hunted up passages from books she would never have heard of, underlined them and sent them to her with a messenger boy who asked no questions and worked cheap. (But I don't have the head to read anything by Thomas Merton today, she told him, and besides I haven't quite finished El Duque de Rivas. You sent him over the day before yesterday, don't you remember? I'm not the intellectual you needed me to be, Martín. I'm more, I don't know, more . . . visual.)

All that was bad. Worse was what he said to her. Such as the fact that he loved her. He had made the greatest blunder of his life in not pursuing her the way he should have, married or single. The night he heard she was engaged to Julio he should have challenged that self-satisfied *criollo* capitalist to a duel. Martín would have won because his father had insisted he learn how to handle a gun and even bought him a brace of expensive Smith & Wesson pistols for his twelfth birthday. (The part about the pistols might have been true; he remembered two of them in a wooden case in his bedroom growing up, though it could have been the attic.) Alas, he loved her. The real reason he had stayed behind in Bolivia when his parents pulled out was to be on the same continent with her, living in the same country, to walk the same cobbled streets of the same unique mountain city as she, to know as he strolled on the Prado that she herself might have crossed the same square of pavement the same day, an hour or a day earlier. It was the pain of proximity that had kept him so resolutely away from her. When they did bump up against one another—at a dinner party, a barbecue in the country at someone's ranch, on the Prado—the long sharp knives of regret and longing pierced him through and through, and he made up his mind not to put himself in that painful position again.

It disturbed him that he was not able to distinguish, despite the rigor with which he thought it through, how much of what he told Montserrat was true.

For better or worse, there was enough of his old analytical self left to be keenly aware of the effect his strange, frenzied courting of Montserrat was having on the object of his obsession. He heard it in the repressed shudder, the drawn-in breath when she picked up the telephone and realized it was he on the other end. He saw it in the unsuccessful way she dissembled in his presence; her hands, always an honest gauge of what was going on inside the woman, invariably gave her away. They twisted and wrung, rubbed and chafed and generally expressed the discomfort she was too kind, or too well bred, to show openly. This will pass, she was saying to the mirror as she brushed her hair in the morning. (She would be wearing a simple, elegant nightgown, off-white, and her age-flecked black hair lay loose on her shoulders, and something feminine, a pin or a comb or some other unnecessary appurtenance of beauty, would be clenched between her perfect teeth as she vigorously worked the brush.) If I humor him, if I stay calm, this strange fit of puppy love in an old dog will spend itself and things will get back to normal, and I may even look forward to running into him around town, once in a while, and we will both enjoy the little secret that exists between us, that he once lost his intellectual head over me.

Either that or she had a friend, a confidante to whom she told everything: every last, humiliating detail of Don Martín del Valle's outlandish behavior. The two of them laughed and commiserated over tea in the big house in Sopocachi. They wondered aloud how a man of his fiber could let himself go so completely. It must have been the solitude, so many years without a woman to keep him sane.

After every outburst of passion, each new incident in which once again he made a fool of himself for Montserrat, he promised himself it was the last. If he was going crazy, he would do so alone. The face he showed to a critical world would be serene, the picture of control; a perfect mask. Then, as if an evil double of himself set out to prove who was really in charge, he called her again, or sent something she didn't want with the trusty messenger, or set out to shop in Little Miami and wound up instead ringing her doorbell in Sopocachi.

This can't go on, he told himself, but no sense of inevitable future reckoning had any power to check him. This can't go on, Montserrat told him daily; my patience is wearing thin, and even if it doesn't you'll wind up hating me for being the only witness to whatever madness this is that you're going through.

Then they cut down his tree.

The crime occurred at night, a week or ten days after the hummingbird threw itself against his window. Dreaming feverishly, when Martín woke he thought the sounds of thrashing and soughing he heard were part of the dream, back into which he was eager to return. But in the morning there it was: chopped dead with a meter of stump left standing, the felled trunk looking as if it had been dead forever, the leaves curling dry, the bonelike twigs sagging earthward.

Martín's father had planted the tree the year he built the house, and Martín had assigned himself the labor of its care. He counted its flourishing among the accomplishments of his life.

Staring at the felled tree, around which an aura of life was still faintly perceptible though fading in the harsh sunlight, he lost track of time. When he came to himself he carried a wrought-iron lawn chair out next to the murdered tree and cried a wake's worth.

That afternoon when the phone bleated into the silence of his grief he ignored it. He was worn out, sucked dry, not enough words left inside to hold up his end of the most trivial conversation. It rang twenty times. Then, a half hour later it started in again. He counted nineteen rings before he picked it up.

"It has to do with justice."

"It has to do with ignorance," he corrected the voice, which gloated. "Savagery and ignorance. There is no more deadly combination on the planet."

"How much have they paid you to write that column?"

Martín could tell, by a certain credulity, that the man had an unrealistic sense of what *El Diario* was willing to pay for opinions the publisher assumed, incorrectly as it happened, supported his own view of the world, which was indeed reactionary. Martín had never done the calculation but assumed that "In the Shadow of the Martyr's Bones" might cover what he drank, in a month, in coffee.

"What do you want from me? To cause me pain? If that's the case you've succeeded. Is there more? Do you want to hear me weep into the receiver?"

"What I want is for you to acknowledge your error. Otherwise . . ."

"Otherwise what?"

"Justice is incomplete, and therefore less satisfying."

"My error, if that's the word you like, was in assuming that the experience of rational discourse would stimulate a few people to challenge their convictions."

"Listen, old man, it's not over. Not yet."

"I suppose it isn't," Martín admitted, defeatism temporarily overmastering him, but the man who had caused his tree to be cut down had already hung up.

He spent the remainder of the afternoon reconstructing in memory a halcyon trip on which he had accompanied a group of wealthy *paceños* up the Mamoré River in 1969. They were the guests of one of the big ranchers in the Beni, whose grandfather had been a rubber baron of sorts back when that particular raw material commanded serious money. The flat-bottomed riverboat was christened *Pride of My Heart*, and among the passengers were Montserrat and Julio. She appeared on the deck each morning wearing a new outfit, and every outfit had something purple about it: a sash, a ribbon, the blouse. It was the kind of attention-drawing whim she was known for in her circle and now, this many years too late, Martín recognized the nature of her genius, which was personal, not replicable, a talent that existed in and for the moment. She was right; he was obtuse.

That night when he called she told him she was traveling the next day to São Paulo, where Julio had left some untidy real-estate investments she had decided to liquidate. He knew she was lying to him, and that the transparency of her lie would give her away. That certainty emboldened him, and he told her again that he loved her. She told him he was worse than a fool, he was pigheaded and willful. He wished he could tell her about his murdered tree, and the vitriolic phone call, but he knew that the telling would disconcert her or, worse, put her on the alert.

The next day Serapio called and Martín put him off, but when his anonymous adversary checked in with him later that same day Martín felt a satisfaction he admitted was perverse. The man's Spanish had that feathery Aymara accent to it, one of the sweetest vocal expressions on the continent, a musical Spanish that was the aural equivalent of home, a place of rest. We should not be enemies,

Martín was unable to bring himself to say to his accuser, we are in fact what your rhetoric would make us: brothers of a sort. Instead he put up with the badgering that seemed to give the man such pleasure. It was a curious blend of old-style Trotskyite political analysis and deeply suspicious xenophobia and something else, less easily pigeonholed, a profound and reverent fatalism, perhaps, the source of which Martín was smart enough not to pretend to understand.

He deliberately lost track of the days. Montserrat did not leave La Paz, of course. He was learning; at least he thought he was. The lie had been as close as she could come, in good conscience, to an enticement. Martín's life lost its familiar outline of days and domestic events, of columns planned and written, quotations recalled and unearthed, of diligent study and homely habits of shopping and puttering, gardening and cleaning. And of brooding, a bad habit he acquired without noticing until it was ingrained in him. He made no move to have the dead tree removed from his back patio. It lay there like the final and conclusive proof of an argument whose shape he was only beginning to make out, now that he was marginally less obtuse.

In place of what he knew, what he was used to knowing, came a curious turmoil of potent dreams and fantastic, almost surreal visits in Sopocachi with Montserrat, who seemed to be growing distinguishably younger, although that could have been a trick his eyes played on him, and painfully long telephone harangues with the man whom Martín could think of only as his adversary, the man sent by heaven or the fates to call him to task.

Midway through a particularly elongated and unusually personal session in which his adversary seemed to have before him a folder with the clips of every last column Martín had ever written, or intended to write, and quoted from them freely, he thought the end to his writer's block (which was really a thinker's block) had finally arrived. It was late evening. The sun had already taken its quota of light westward above the lip of the canyon, and La Paz doubled itself in shadow. It was a time of day that gave Martín particular pleasure, brought out his best thoughts. His adversary was quoting at tedious length a 1975 column in which he apparently had analyzed the rhetoric of a campaign speech given by one of the mining union leaders and found it wanting in Cartesian logic. Pleasant as it was, the man's voice droned as he enumerated the sins against solidarity Martín had committed in the piece. And suddenly there it was, the title for his next column: "The Insufficiency of Ideology."

Phrases, finally, came crowding into his distracted mind, and he searched for paper and pencil to jot them down as he listened. It was all there, white germ and the black dirt to grow it, lacking only the hours of effort that would make the prose bloom in rainbow colors.

"You know the one thing I really can't forgive you, del Valle?" his adversary wanted to know.

"Tell me, please."

"That you hate it."

"Hate what?"

"Our country, Bolivia."

He waited to be corrected, but Martín was too stubborn to give him the truth that might absolve him in the man's mind: that his love for the country of his birth was a staggering thing, almost too much, sometimes, to bear. It manifested itself in the details, the namable particulars that assaulted his eyes every day: the stones of the streets of La Paz, the radiant faces of two *cholita* sisters placid and beautiful together on a street corner before the work day began, the wild mountains and the wilder sky that held them in place, the way water coursed through the gutters of his city like muddy silver during a hard rain. He could lose himself listing the particulars, but he refused to prostitute that love to convince his adversary he was not guilty as charged.

Eventually the man hung up.

"Your phone's been busy all evening," Montserrat observed sharply when he got through to her. He hadn't realized his fingers were dialing.

"I was talking," he explained, "to a friend. That's what you call a person who makes you aware of your faults, isn't it, a friend? But you called me . . ." A first.

"Only to tell you that the trip to São Paulo is back on."

"Do you remember that trip up the Mamoré, back in 1969?"

"Vaguely. Where do you stay when you go to São Paulo?"

"Do you remember the canoe?"

"What canoe? You're babbling, Martín. I'm concerned for you."

"We went upstream exploring a little tributary river. Julio was gone, fishing and drinking with the other men."

"Please don't make something up. Your memory makes me uneasy."

"We paddled until we came to a kind of a glade, a dry spot of higher ground. I remember banks of the most extraordinary flowers. We sat in the grass in the glade, on a blanket, actually. The sun was fierce, but there was a little breeze that dried the sweat on our skin."

"Birds landed in my hair," she said, so softly he had a hard time catching the words.

"White," he reminded her. "Like a dove except smaller."

"Did I tell you that Julio used to run around on me? Almost from the beginning. Love dies, doesn't it? That's just what happens. You learn to live with absence."

"I love you, Montserrat."

"So what do you propose? That we lie down together and pretend?"

"Touch would be enough, maybe. Touching. And talking. At least to start with."

"Tell me what you remember about those birds, please. The doves."

"They weren't doves, they were too small to be doves. I never did learn the proper name for them but they were splendid creatures, like *mistura*, confetti in the air thrown by a very strong hand."

"Martín?"

"Yes?"

"I think I'm starting to remember now."

His dreaming ceased that night, as if for good, and in the morning Martín went out back to pick flowers to take to Montserrat. He had almost become used to the carcass of the martyr's bones tree lying crosswise in the spongy, damp grass of his patio sanctuary. He wanted a perfect bouquet. The choosing was pure pleasure, and he took his time about it, so that he was not inside his living room when it exploded.

The force of the blast, however, picked him up and threw him backward several meters. He landed on his back next to a flowering kantuta and lost consciousness for a few moments. When he came to himself and understood that the front of his house no longer existed, he was first awed and then overwhelmed by a flitting vision of the world's knowledge that went flying up in a cloud of smoky destruction. All those books, burning page by page or simply obliterated, undone and unbecome. There went Aquinas and Augustine. He saw, in his brief vision, the flaming end of Borges and Adolfo Becquer and Walt Whitman and Flaubert and Katherine Anne Porter. In the sudden, swift intensity of their going he had the impression that they might all be shrieking together, but his senses jangled, his body hurt badly, and he could be sure of nothing.

Except that Montserrat had indeed always preferred her roses with long stems. That much he remembered. He got to his knees. The joints ached. He got to his feet. He was aware, peripherally, that he still had a kitchen, which meant coffee. And rose bushes in tended abundance. There were his clippers lying in the grass, tossed when the blast knocked him down. Sunlight glinted on the blades. He bent slowly, picked up the clippers, and went to work. You learn to live with absence, she had said. But proximity was a good beginning, touch and talk. The day promised to be fine. With a little luck the air would be full of small, white, dovelike birds. He didn't dare raise his eyes to see, not just yet. But rather than take a taxi he thought he might walk from Miraflores to Sopocachi.

down in paraguay

In an inert suburb of Asunción the bats had begun to sweep and curry the violet air of early evening. The sun had sunk like a hunk of glowing lead. Under a hairy-boled palm a fat American in a blue Hawaiian shirt stood and sweated. He looked more surreptitious than discreet. His hands were clasped behind his substantial back; the stylized palm trees on his shirt stretched at the belly. As he studied the windows of a tidy pink stucco house across the sandy way, a neighborhood band began to practice at the far end of the street. What they wanted was a popular waltz, but the accordion lost its way immediately.

The music disturbed the watching man's concentration. He could not ignore it. The insincere expression of equanimity on his face was that of a senile lion. The short bristles of a brown mustache stood straight out, the brown eyes squinted slightly. As the band meandered through several false starts on its way to the waltz he cocked his head to one side; it was no good. Each time the accordion wandered from the hackneyed track of the waltz, and the music stopped sputteringly.

As he watched, the American was composing a letter to a friend in the States. He was not sure to whom he would send the letter when he actually put pencil to paper, but the process of mental drafting forced him to clarify certain difficult thoughts.

. . . *As I understand Paraguayan law, I don't actually have to nab the two of them in the act. If the . . . abuse is blatant I can be legally provoked by less.*

Abuse was not the word he wanted, but a better would come.

. . . *Would you expect a diesel mechanic, U.S. Navy retired, to follow the fine points of South American law? You would not. But two Stateside divorces taught me a little, anyway. Here it's different. Here a man has the rights that go along with having balls. Don't read me wrong, though. I'm not out to pull some macho stunt. I can explain this to you because you are a friend and will catch my drift: When I think about killing the guy I get scared as hell. If I didn't have to, I wouldn't.*

The accordion player finally found his place. The familiar regular music of the waltz revolved slowly in the purple air, in which the smell of something like sex hung like rotting mangoes. Not a smell precisely but an air itself, wet and heavy and all smoothed into the purple atmosphere he breathed. Perhaps it wasn't sex at all but something like it that closed about the man, making him tense and nostalgic, sad and awake at once. For a single notched instant, he felt as though he could see clearly both his past and his future, and the same wild longing frustrated both.

. . . *I married her in good faith, you see. At first I thought the little kid tagging along was really her brother. But when I figured it out I said to her just don't lie to me. You made a mistake. You want to hear about mistakes listen to me, I'm the screw-up king of the Western Hemisphere. You screwed up and you paid the price. If we get married I'll adopt him. Just don't lie to me. I like little Pancho. I call him hey Pancho and I make him call me Cisco even though he doesn't get the joke. On Sundays we go out hunting in the country. I gave him the .22 my old man gave me. First son and all that business. I went through all the rigmarole of adopting him, which was my first taste of Paraguayan law. Just don't lie to me, I told his mother.*

From the direction of the waltz a slight figure came glidingly to join him.

"Hola, Cisco."

"Hey, Pancho. You better go hunt up your friends or something, buddy."

The boy shook his head. "Are you going to kill him, Cisco?"

"Kill who?"

"Don't treat me like a kid," the boy said quietly, wounded at any condescension. "You know who I mean. My mother has disgraced both of us. You do not hear the gossiping, but I can hear nothing else. If you do not kill him, I will."

"You keep out of this, little one."

"How?"

When the fat man did not answer, Pancho drew a heavy-handled silver knife from his waist and offered it to him.

"Now what do you suppose that's for?" the American mused.

No response. The knife lay in Pancho's upturned palms, an acolyte's offering to the celebrant. With its stubby blade it looked like a toy.

As the American deliberated, the sound of a man softly whistling made itself heard in the gaps in the practice waltz. A light in the front-room window of the pink house was turned on at the same time. Pancho and his adoptive father watched: a white shirt, black pants, broad-brimmed sombrero pulled low to hide the face. No shoes. A sauntering whistle. The door of the house opened halfway, a woman stepped into the patio, and the knife passed as if unconsciously into the American's hand.

"Now. Do it now," Pancho whispered. "If you need proof, there it is."

"Wait. Let's see what happens."

In a yellow flowered dress that made her look slatternly and sweetly domestic at the same time, the woman loitered coyly among the flowers of the patio. Nervous. She snapped a white rose from a bush the American had planted; she fastened it into her hair with a pin she had been holding in her mouth.

With a petulant whine, the male voice told her to hurry. Opening the gate into the street halfway, just as far as she had opened the door of the house, the woman in yellow appeared in the sandy street. The American recognized the air she wore like a shawl about her person: Her presence alone was a concession, it meant a prize any man with life in his veins would die to win.

One hand on Pancho's shoulder in a fatherly gesture, the American whispered to the boy, "I want to see where they go."

The strain of expecting reminded him of the way it was, sometimes, when they were hunting, when Pancho was too eager to kill something.

"Then let's go."

"I'm going alone, son."

"You can't. You won't do it. You'll forgive her or something."

"I'll do what has to be done. Make yourself scarce, Pancho. Or you and me are quits. You got that?"

His father's untypical harshness startled Pancho into obeying; perhaps the American finally meant business.

"*Suerte,*" he said slowly, and he was gone.

At a safe distance the American in the Hawaiian shirt began tracking his Paraguayan wife and the sombrero. His feet kicked heavily through the sand; walking on sand always fatigued him. The sweat had dried on his skin, and he felt a chill as though a breeze had come up.

. . . *Before we got married I tried to tell her how it was with me. Double-barreled alimony blows the hell out of my pension check. Forget that, I said. On what's left we can get drunk once a week if we're lucky. And I showed her exactly what the shop brings in. But she wouldn't believe me. She was sure I had big money salted away somewhere. She wanted a rich*

North American, so she closed her eyes and said it was me. Pretty nervy when you think about it, especially with Pancho and all.

The purple air was growing inky, jets of black seeping into the spongy sky. The night would be tremendously still and dark, the kind of night that brought on dreams. At a corner he sensed the direction they had gone and followed doggedly, trying not to shuffle. He forgot the knife, which he had slipped into a pocket. It made him sick to think of her going with the sombrero to a public place in their own neighborhood.

. . . It's a proven fact (proven by me) that some guys have no luck at all picking women. My first one was young, eighteen or so. She wanted money, too. Damn but I never had any. She wanted a Buick, one of those big limo types with leather all over the inside. At the time I was a petty officer and I had to ship out all the time. It was in the cards, I guess. She had two little girls by me, just for the support money it turns out. Then she started throwing things at me when I came home. After a while every last thing in the house was busted, and still no Buick.

Mortification like a spasm hit him when he realized that they were strolling boldly toward an outdoor restaurant, Los Tres Chiflados. As he watched them open the gate he heard more waltzing. "Brazen bitch," he said aloud.

. . . You'd think the first time I got burned would have taught me to keep my hand out of the fire, but it didn't. The second time I went for age and stability. She was thirty-seven, I was about thirty. So, what happens? I come home by surprise one night and there she is in the sack with a hillbilly musician. The damn electric guitar was in bed with them. This long curled black cord came running out from beneath the covers into a little amplifier and she was stroking them strings for all it was worth. You'd think the courts would have made her pay me for the pain and suffering I went through, but there's no justice in Gringolandia.

. . . Living down here is different. Hard to explain if you haven't seen it firsthand. One weekend Pancho and I were out camping, hunting. The first night we went to sleep early. But in the middle of the night we heard a big row and got up to check it out. A big moon the color of cloudy

pisswater was out, making everything around look smooth and phony, as
though there was a coat of bright enamel over everything.

. . . The noise was coming from a gully where there had been a fire not
too long before. Me and Pancho stood on the edge of the gully and looked
down. Nothing but charred trunks. In the moonlight the place looked like
the moon, if you can picture the moon with burnt trees on it. In the middle
of the gully, though, we saw this wildcat tearing up the carcass of some
other animal it had dragged down. It was going crazy from the blood and
the meat and the smell and all. I mean crazy as in crazy. It was leaping up
and down to beat the band and tearing into that dead thing in a horrible
way, like killing and eating it wasn't enough.

. . . Anyhow, something about that night—the burnt-up gully and the
sick piss moon and the wildcat leaping up—grabbed me. In its own way it
made some kind of sense. And I had the feeling that I had been there before,
watching it happen and thinking it made sense. Still have. If I close my
eyes sometimes it's all there, and it makes sense. Hell, that isn't what I was
trying to say. That doesn't begin to tell you what I mean to say about this
place. Does it?

He broke off the letter because his thoughts were not steady on
their feet. They skated like the puddles of grease on the soup his
wife gave him every day at lunch.

There could be no more evasion. Friends of his or at least neighbors would be there inside Los Tres Chiflados. A fence and grape-
vine blocked his view. But there could be no more evasion.

When a small boy came by he gave him some change and told
him to tell the sombrero and the woman he was with that a friend
from old times was waiting in the street. Incurious, the boy took the
money and slipped through the front gate.

Tonight there was no moon, and the blue-black sky was blotched
with the denser black mass of running clouds. The air was tolerably
cool for summer and the city. The band left the waltz and tumbled
into a polka, though it was early for anyone to dance. The gate
opened, and there was the sombrero. Behind it came the American's
wife, her air of housewifely sexuality on display in a way that cut.

The situation shaped itself quickly, almost too quickly for anger. They both recognized him; he saw it in the way they stiffened. On its own volition Pancho's knife made a tearing stab. The sombrero ran, and she fell quickly. She made no sound, gave no signal, as though by her cooperation she acknowledged her fault in the mess. The yellow dress he hated went black with blood, which also stained the sand.

Before any consequences there would be a break, a hiatus that did not depend entirely on waiting. Overhead the black clouds tore. The polka music cavorted like a clown on big feet, and a drunk inside the fence laughed. No purple, no sex, no remembering cluttered the cool air. He knelt beside her. There was an interval of tender conjugal intimacy that was only partly sad. While it lasted, he tried with deliberate slowness to figure out whether he had known when he took the knife that this—precisely this—was the way it was going to turn out. No answer. He wondered, too, what had become of the white rose in her hair. No answer. As he noticed that the polka music was ending and someone who would see them was stepping through the restaurant gate, he was pretty sure that there was no answer.

dove of the
back streets

On the morning of her fifty-fifth birthday Katrina Webern woke to the voices. She had endured a long silence, long enough to despair of ever hearing them again. *One loses the voices as she ages, my dear,* she imagined her mother saying, tapping her daughter's forearm with a fat finger of admonition. If her mother had lived long enough to instruct her in such matters. Katrina's seven dogs and nine cats fretted around the house wanting food and attention. Never mind. She lay on her back on top of her big brass bed listening to the voices. Thank God she had oiled the ceiling fan. It stirred the stifling humid air of January with quiet efficiency. Though she sweated she was not tremendously uncomfortable, and nothing distracted her from the perfect pleasure of the voices. The normal sex hunger of morning was there, as constant as money was short. But neither the name nor the face of Douglas Fairbanks Rodriguez occurred, just then, to torment her. She luxuriated in the voices.

As was her custom, she converted what she heard into a story: A family was traveling by sleigh through the Black Forest. The tinkle of the sleigh bells was muffled; the horses snorted in the cold; the runners sliced the crisp snow. Dr. Webern, good soul, was on his way to attend to a medical emergency in a remote village. Because it was Christmas Eve he took his family along. When he was done with his business they would stop at an inn he frequented and drink mulled wine with cinnamon, toasting the birth of their Savior and the vanquishing of evil. Swaddled in wool in the sleigh, in awe of the untinctured black surrounding them, a young girl rode in her mother's lap. There was no difference in what the girl saw eyes open, eyes closed. Around her the voices ran like water, the individual words blurred to sounds of comfort and reassurance, bass and baritone and soprano noises in patterned harmony such as the quiet gods made among themselves talking over the shape of the universe they were about to create. There was no end to the ride through the dark woods, no end to the river of sound or to the girl's acute delight.

There were ways and ways of telling a story, each as accurate as the next because all of them contained the truth of a particular moment. Dashing Douglas was the only one to whom she had confided the version of the story in which the little girl had never actually been to Germany. She was born in Paraguay after her parents fled Hitler's enthusiasms in the thirties. In the vicious jungle life in which she was reared that was cause for pride and consolation, that Dr. Webern had been sickened by what he saw happening in his homeland and fled before the disease infected his family. Not many could say as much. In her moments of maximum discouragement the knowledge kept Katrina's head held high.

When the voices faded she pulled on her Chinese silk robe and fed the animals. The sick duck a neighbor had dropped off looked fat and happy, cured by music. Each species tended to respond to a specific form, although there were exceptions. Cats liked chamber music, dogs preferred symphonies. The duck was an opera buff, which discrimination endeared the animal to her and guaranteed it a long, unthreatened life under her roof. How could you eat a creature that thrived on arias?

The animals attended, she made tea and drank it outside under her grapefruit tree. The blue enameled tin of English breakfast tea had been a present from the German ambassador, who often brought her tokens on the major national holidays. A delicacy, she assured him as she accepted the gift, so that the discomfort he felt at her straitened circumstances did not spoil the visit for either of them. Looking around the yard as she sipped the sweet hot tea, she understood that a bureaucrat from Bonn might well feel a certain squeamishness, and she forgave him the impulse to recoil he never completely hid. Partly it was the fierce climate, which caused leaves and limbs to drop and rot, and paint to peel, and grass to parch, and women to wither and waste, so that the green patio and the little wooden house on the lip of the Paraguay River seemed always to be a litter, caught in a messy transition between birth and unbecoming. Besides which the animals stank. She couldn't help that.

The return of the voices had put her in a good mood. Her fence was high and the neighbors indifferent. She was tempted to throw off her robe and dance in her underwear to an Italian folk tune that had lately been in her head. Who cared what a middle-aged German woman might look like in the buff? Those large, round, pink-nippled breasts had suckled only men, no children. Those blue-veined calves, those plump, dimpled arms ought to make a man think of health and pleasure and yes, sexual ecstasy. A few pounds less and her classic *alemana* face would suggest again what it always had, a striking combination of intelligence and passion brought to a perfect pitch of cultured feeling when she opened her mouth on the stage and sang. She felt sweat trickle underneath her left breast. She did not dance.

The neighbor's dull son Alejandro, whom she called Alexis because she knew it irritated him, called over the fence that she had a telephone call. One of her students would have been deputized to let her know what she already knew, that they wanted to offer her a birthday party at the conservatory. A small act of homage was how they would describe it. She would not disappoint them. She pulled the tasseled rope of her pale blue robe tight, shoved her feet into sandals, and went down the dirt-and-grass street to Alejandro's house to take the call.

★ ★ ★

"It's not me." She shook her head. "It's you. It's your love and labor, your passion and your dedication that make the magic. Remember, please, why it is we call this humble hall, these modest walls, a conservatory. Remember we are conserving, for ourselves and for those who come after us, something that the world would just as soon ignore, or discard, or even destroy, something called culture."

Conscious of her timing, she looked around the room at each of their sober faces in turn. This much at least they deserved: recognition that the effort with which they fortified their dreams was holy. Because it was. In a violent jungle world—a world like Asunción—culture stood the same chance as a lamb in a pit against an unbaptized lion. As she caught her breath and her congregation waited with rapt patience, lips moving silently she itemized the constituent elements of their world, which was perilously close, on the bad days, to her own: sweat and chronic shortage and a blind striving for satisfaction that was not to be had. Heat and damp decay and a perpetual effort to dull the hunger for beauty with substitutes like alcohol and noise and anger, none of which accomplished their purpose. She could go on. Better not to.

Unbidden, Rosa Maria rose from her seat to deliver a testimonial Katrina did not have the heart to reject. Pale and awkward when she was not dancing, her round face with a tendency to sag in repose, the girl was grace itself when she performed. Her clunky, overweight mother clutched a soiled vinyl purse to her breast in a vain effort to conceal her pride in the angel of motion to whom she had given birth sixteen years ago.

"*Profesora*," Rosa Maria said formally. "I am confident I speak for all of us when I say that we would be nothing without you and your guidance. Your wisdom. You are . . ." She searched for an adequate image. "You are the angel who comes into a dark room and switches on the light so that the plain people can see."

She sat down quickly as heads nodded in approval both of the sentiment and of the felicity with which it was expressed, and Katrina wished her own gratitude toward her pupils could be as clean and uncomplicated as theirs toward her. Instead she felt bitterness rise and spread through her body, up into her throat where it was converted into words she would be a fool to utter. It was the place itself, perhaps: the water-stained plaster walls, the mismatched pair of grating pole fans that did nothing to relieve the unbearable heat. The disruptive groans of buses going by in the street. The reddish grime collected on the posters and pictures no matter how frequently they were dusted, so that you when you walked into the conservatory in the morning it was like entering a tomb. Here—if a person knew how to look for them—lay buried her own dreams.

The *sidra*, sparkling cider with just enough alcohol in it to take the rough edge off an occasion like this one, was waiting in a champagne bucket in which the ice melted quickly. The celebration could be squandered if she let herself go into a slide. Only something lovely could save them, and only Katrina du Champs was lovely enough. But Katrina needed just a little time to come up with a convincing anecdote, so she invited Hector to the piano, where he butchered—poor talentless soul—"*Für Elise*" to the great satisfaction of the assembly (although Katrina was relieved to see Rosa Maria wince, which led her mother to scowl at her). A small, wide man with a smile that sought to overcome nervousness by ingratiating, Hector was in point of fact a butcher. He worked for the German cooperative on Avenida España, hacking away at dead cows twelve hours a day. How could Katrina deny him such consolation as he could coax from an instrument he attacked the way he took on a side of bloody beef?

After leading the applause for *"Für Elise,"* which after all survived the ordeal, Katrina was composed enough to compose. It was Hector himself who requested, with his unfailing ham-handed politeness, that she sing for them, preferably something by her namesake, Katrina du Champs. Katrina nodded. She thought she might do a leider she hadn't done since Buenos Aires, back in the golden years when her soul swelled up inside her body, almost choking her, as she walked downtown to study her name on a marquee.

"How curiously our minds work," she mused aloud. "This morning when I woke and remembered it was my birthday, all I could think of was the strange occurrence that befell Katrina du Champs on her nineteenth birthday."

It pleased her to see how her voice mesmerized them; she mesmerized herself. They knew as well as she the history of the plucky nineteenth-century German girl with a French father who had bested all odds and the hostility of an art world that doubted the intellectual capacity of women to become the most celebrated composer-singer of leider of her time.

What the students couldn't know was what Katrina Webern had not known herself, that on her nineteenth birthday Katrina du Champs had been attacked in the street in Cologne by a deranged admirer. The son of a wealthy barrel manufacturer who had seen her perform, he had become obsessed with her beauty, which was numinous and delicate. She knew he was following her; he had been skulking in her background for weeks. But her mother was dead and her French father had not taken her seriously when she confessed her fear to him. He was, as they knew, a dissolute sot whose consuming goal was to retire to a country place in Alsace on Katrina's earnings and reputation, boasting to people of quality that it was he who had identified and nurtured his daughter's genius. So ugly Hans, the barrel manufacturer's son, stalked until the right moment arrived and then dragged her into a dark alley.

At that point in Katrina's narration, Rosa Maria's mother fished in her purse for a handkerchief, then blew her nose trumpet-fashion, so loudly that everyone in the conservatory jumped in his or her chair. Mortified, her gifted daughter pretended not to notice the wet sobs of sympathy bubbling from her mother's mouth. Katrina was weakened with a flash of sisterly solidarity with the girl, whose fiber was like her own, dangerously fine for the environment in which they were fated to live.

It was August hot in Cologne—the seasons were reversed in the Northern Hemisphere, Katrina explained—so the young composer was lightly dressed. Through her summer jacket, her almond-colored crepe blouse, she felt the man's hands come at her, clawing and pawing, and she resisted. Valiantly. When he saw that she would not surrender to his rough charm, Hans threatened in gutter German to slice the cords in her neck. Submit, was the proposal, or she would never sing again.

Although they knew she must have gotten out of the scrape safely, since she went on to sing in triumph in the principal capitals of Europe, Katrina Webern's students were wrought up at the bestial attack their heroine suffered. Their collective breathing was indignant. Pausing to capture the rest of the story from the mysterious place in which it had its birth, Katrina caught a whiff of the body cologne she had doused herself with at home before boarding the bus to the conservatory, the rent on which she was several months behind. Lavender, that was the smell. It had been a present from a Danish tractor salesman who described how he had been transported to the upper ether once by a concert she gave in Buenos Aires. It was the lavender, for some reason, that provoked the insight: Conserving, the thing one did in a conservatory, was really an act of creation. And invention, at which she excelled, was equally an act of preservation. The difference was unimportant, finally, between making up and making over. What mattered was what one had in her hands, or her heart, or her head, that was worth keeping.

In her discouraged fifties, Katrina was seldom, anymore, on the receiving end of insights worthy of the name. She attributed her luck to the return of the voices after long absence. She needed time to digest what she had just learned, but here was a familiar voice finishing the story of what happened to Katrina du Champs the day she turned nineteen.

All fifteen culture-bedazzled heads in *Profesora* Katrina Webern's Conservatorio de las Bellas Artes turned to the shabby threshold on which he stood, dressed in black and just as beautiful as memory made him. Dashing Douglas Fairbanks Rodriguez. He was supposed to be in Montevideo doing a stage version of a Manuel Puig novel. That, at any rate, had been his cover story.

"Feliz cumpleaños, Profesora Katrina," he said engagingly, bowing in her direction. "I wish you a very happy birthday." Charm dripped from every surface of his lithe and muscled actor's body. Who could believe he would turn thirty-five in a couple more months? Certainly not the mother of Rosa Maria, who stared at the newcomer eyes wide and mouth open like a slow fish suddenly sighting the god of the deeps, the truth of whose existence it had previously doubted. Nor for that matter Rosa Maria herself, who was as flustered as her mother. Her toes tapped the floor instinctively. The reaction that jumped in Katrina was confusing, an impulse to protect colored by jealousy. If anyone was to be despoiled by that terrible manly power, that hurtful beauty, it was she herself, Katrina alone.

"May I?" he asked, cocking his handsome head sideways.

"Of course," she conceded.

He was finishing her story as he came across the room. Hector, in whom Katrina had once confided a little of the pain that Dashing Douglas had caused her in the course of their tumultuous friendship, glowered threateningly toward the ceiling. Douglas was not the sort to notice. For an instant Katrina was distracted by a vision of the earnest, simple-hearted butcher hacking away with a bloody-toothed saw on the carcass of the actor as it dangled from a meat hook in the German cooperative.

"Trapped in a black alley in a part of Cologne she really should not have been walking in alone, Katrina du Champs knew her only recourse was to outsmart the bully Hans, who rode his father's thoroughbred horses in the hills around the Mosel and was as strong as an ox, apart from being a cad. Right so far, *Profesora*? Am I telling the story correctly?"

He was telling it correctly. He took his place next to her on the small plywood platform she liked to think of as the pulpit from which she professed her faith in culture, faced the students in their folding chairs, bowed again just the right amount to acknowledge their attention, which was undividedly his to savor.

"Well. What could she do? What would you have done?"

Maria Magdalena, a young woman whose outstanding features were her elbows and knuckles and who had saved two and a half years to buy a secondhand flute from a pawnshop facing the cemetery in Luque, looked as though she was willing to venture a guess as to what she would have done in Katrina du Champs's circumstances that night in Cologne. She brushed the limp brown hair from her face, fidgeting in her seat, but by the time she was completely sure of her response Douglas was answering his own question.

"Allowing her body to slump, as though she were too exhausted or too terrified to fight off the son of the barrel manufacturer any longer, she began to sing."

Wonderful. The expressions on the students' faces, the ease and satisfaction their bodies radiated, told Katrina he had hit the mark dead center. Stupendous. But she was not about to let him walk away with her story. She nodded vigorously and picked up the thread she had dropped. "Miss du Champs writes in her memoirs— I hope someday they are translated into Spanish; if I had the money I would do it myself, so that you could enjoy them the way I have for all these years—she writes that her mind simply drew a blank.

She could not come up with a single tune, a single word from her extensive repertoire. Nothing, not even a nursery rhyme."

Douglas, the bastard, watched her with evident admiration. She registered that his raven hair was longer than he used to wear it, and that he had cut himself shaving. In actor's black he was sinister and radiant.

"Still, she knew she must sing," Katrina continued, "and when she opened her mouth out came a leider, brand new and brilliant, the words perfectly matched with the music. It was a song she later sang in Vienna under the title of "Dove of the Back Streets," and witnesses who were there on opening night claimed that the hardboiled critic in the front row cried. At any rate, when Hans heard the extraordinary music that came out of her mouth he let her go. He slunk out of the alley without a word and never bothered her again. And Katrina, shaken but awfully relieved, as you might imagine, rushed home to the protection of her father. Such as it was."

What the world that counted, the world that knew how to judge these things, would never know was just how good Katrina Webern's leider was. Her rendition of "Dove on the Back Streets" for the assembled students and for Dashing Douglas was an extraordinary invention. Some of those listening perceived, to a certain extent, the brilliance. Rosa Maria, for one, and Douglas, and a few of the others, whose taste was on a higher plane than their abilities. The Cologne story helped, putting Katrina in the proper frame of mind so that she became herself the terrified young girl accosted by a fiend who threatened to cut her vocal cords, and with them, the lifeline to her dreams. The story of the dove flapped up and out the way the composer's had, from a place she thought of as inside simply to give it a location. The applause was as close to deafening as sixteen people in a small hall could make it.

"You're not coming home with me," she whispered angrily to Douglas the first chance she got while they drank their *sidra* and ate the flaky guayaba pastries Rosa Maria's mother had made for the party. "Never again, so don't try anything funny."

He raised his eyebrows but refused to be offended. There was no way, short of a scandal she could not abide, to stop him from boarding the bus with her for the long ride out to the little town on the bank of the river where she had found a piece of property cheap enough to have a house of sorts.

"What happened in Montevideo?" she asked him after the first noisy, stop-and-go kilometer on the bus.

A bricklayer in the seat ahead of them turned around rudely to stare. He had been drinking, and the smell of cane whiskey polluted the space between them. In Buenos Aires, in the golden era of Katrina's success, she had been picked up by a driver and taken to the theater. Granted, he was a taxi driver from the provinces who smelled of garlic, but the impresario had paid for the service for as long as the show ran, which was not as long as it should have. His mistake was billing her as a Paraguayan rather than a German. The Argentine critics attended the opening night performance with their minds made up: The novelty of a leider singer from the Paraguayan jungle might make good copy for a day or two, but she could not possibly be up to the level they deserved in the capital of Latin American culture.

Douglas shrugged. She knew from experience that he disliked it when her mind wandered in his presence; he was, or ought to be, fascination enough. "I saw your face everywhere I turned, Katrina Webern. In Montevideo. I was obsessed. Just like Hans the barrel boy."

"They fired you."

A similar shrug. Manfully he fought the irritation he wanted to take out on her. "Call it a creative disagreement. I mean between their vision of what the play was supposed to be and mine. Mine was better. Mine was cleaner. Mine was brilliant."

Of course. That much could well be true. She glared down the bricklayer, who turned away, cleaned the blade of his trowel with a thick, dirty thumbnail.

"There's nothing left to pawn, Douglas," she warned him.

"I came home for love, Katrina, not for consumer goods."

Her birthday ruined, she got up and moved to an empty seat on the other side of the bus.

At home the sun was going down splashily, streaks and whorls of cloud-enhanced color making the horizon on the river briefly sublime. Clouds of mosquitoes formed in the wet, heavy air, fish jumped and plunked, and a whole summer's worth of *cigarra* bugs expressed their sense of being alive in coordinated crescendoes of mournful sound. It was a bad habit, but Katrina wondered what the weather was like in Germany just then. The world, she lectured herself, was what you saw when you opened your eyes, the dirt you dug your toes into, it was the soup of smells that assaulted your nose when what you wanted was clean. Germany was an insidious abstraction.

Her animals clamored for her attention. Half a dozen of them tangled their legs around hers as she hunted through the refrigerator for a treat she could stretch to feed all of them. She hummed a nonsense piece in German while Douglas puttered around the house looking for something to fix. And then they were there again, the voices, notwithstanding the dreadful ending to the day and the presence in her home of a selfish, talented man who had bruised her heart more times than either of them could count. Resting a moment against the side of the refrigerator, for the coolness, she listened to the voices run. No story came this time, none needed. It was pure sound, straight from the source. Katrina was a rock, and the voices were the river flowing around the rock, around it, as if forever.

The animals fed, to make it easy on Douglas she slipped away through the patio, out the back gate, followed the grassy track to a bluff overlooking the river that was as good as private property since no one ever came there. She was sweating terribly from the bus ride and all that trudging in the heat. The air was still, not even a finger of wind to move it anywhere. She slipped out of her dress and sat in her camisole in the stiff, high grass looking at the river, which was quickly turning black. If a person went far enough on that placid, dark surface she would wind up in Buenos Aires. How could that be? It was the voices, she decided, that were making her feel melancholy. She was out of the habit of hearing.

She wondered what Douglas would choose to take. She had said there was nothing to pawn, but that was true only in an emotional sense. In fact his artist's eye would be drawn to what was left of her mother's jewelry, which would be a shame since he wouldn't get a tenth of what it was worth; she knew that from having tried herself. There was a fine Russian icon her father had picked up on a trip to Moscow once, and a jeweled dagger and a gold candlestick from Istanbul. And some Chinese ivory her father had particularly favored. She hoped Douglas would have the sense to insist on fair value for whatever it was he decided on. In downtown Asunción was a Jewish woman who had survived the Holocaust and had the tattooed number to prove it. She loved to speak German with Katrina. They discussed their favorite operas, and the thoroughgoing corruption in Paraguayan politics, and the voracious destruction of the rainforest in Brazil to the north. The woman scrupulously gave fair value. Katrina hoped Douglas would take her property to her.

But here he was at the river, and empty-handed. "You're a vision, Katrina Webern," he told her, sinking onto the grass. "Did you think you could run away from me?"

"I'm fifty-five today, Douglas, and the world I needed to live in is a long way away, and all you've ever done is hurt me."

He put his arm around her shoulders. "There's probably not another multilingual blond woman in a thousand-kilometer radius who's going gray as gracefully as you. You'll be attractive as long as you live, Katrina, and you know it."

"My mother told me just how badly a man could hurt a woman, Douglas. My father was the exception. All that racist rant in the streets of Germany, all that hate he saw around him, used to make him physically sick. He came home and threw up in the toilet. Time and again. Him, a doctor who had to cut diseased limbs off suffering people."

"Your mother died when you were seven, didn't she? I can't believe she would have poisoned you like that against men in general, not from what you've told me about the woman."

"Douglas?"

"*Che*, I oiled the fan for you."

There was no oil in the house; she had borrowed some from the neighbors and returned the container.

"Will you please go away?" she begged him. "I can't go through it again."

"I was in the theater in Montevideo," he began, and she knew it was going to be the real reason why he would not go away and leave her in peace. "Dress rehearsal for the Puig thing. Just before it began. Everyone was buzzing like bees, caught up in the play and themselves and the magic they were going to make . . ."

"I don't want to hear it," she tried.

"I was by myself in a corner listening to it all, watching them, and I was suddenly overwhelmed with a sense of how trivial it was. All of it, all of them. They were mediocre and they might never know. And I thought of this German woman I knew in Paraguay who had composed songs that should be in the canon, they were so good."

"Stop, please."

"I can't stop, Katrina. I thought, there is no justice in the world, when a woman of genius has to invent a hundred-and-fifty-year-old alter ego and pretend her own work belongs to her so that people who can't appreciate what they hear will listen when she sings."

"You know nothing about Katrina du Champs."

"I know about Katrina Webern," he told her. He eased her out flat in the grass, worked her out of the camisole, and made the most unselfish love to her that he had ever made. It was as though he could see in the dark on the surface of her body just where the hurting parts were located—they must have glowed—and eased them with his hands, the tips of his sensitive fingers, his tongue, which paid the strictest homage.

Afterward they both dozed on the bluff. When they woke he was still gentle, as though he had finally learned to put aside his own clamoring need and give her a gift worth the giving, worth receiving. The moonlight that marbled the still surface of the river in flat patterns made his body into the body of a god, a statue into which Zeus had breathed life. Her own, she imagined, was something like a castle, or an island, or some other special place an intrepid explorer could conquer if he only knew how to get there. She let him dress her up to the camisole, carried her dress over her arm, and they walked back home barefoot together without talking.

"May I stay the night, Katrina?" he wanted to know at the gate.

If she said go he would go away. This was a different Douglas.

"Stay," he told him.

They made a different kind of love in the brass bed, more demanding of both of them, acrobatic and not the least bit romantic. It was like a meal after a long hungry spell, and no need for either of them to apologize for being ravenous. She wondered how many more years she would feel such hunger; she could not conceive of a life without it. If her mother had survived the harshness of Paraguay she would have told her what to expect. Letting down, Douglas wanted to talk about her music, about his acting, about tall talent standing on a small platform and the malicious indifference of a dull world. That, not the difference in their bodies, was what made her feel the gap in their ages, and she shushed him with a hand over his mouth. He licked the hand, grasped her breast, and fell asleep again as though drugged.

It took Katrina longer to sleep. She lay on her back listening to her animals rustle around the house, and a bus brake whistling out near the bridge into Argentina, and several million *cigarra* bugs trying to drown out anything that wasn't them, and fireworks going off distantly that meant somebody's favorite team had scored a goal, and a rooster startled out of a bad dream. But she gave way, eventually, her body pleasantly conscious of Douglas's next to it in the bed that Dr. Webern had shipped from Germany back when he could no longer bear seeing what his people were doing to the Jews. Paraguay had been hard on him, too, though he lasted longer than Katrina's mother. What have I done to you? he asked her wonderingly when she leaned to kiss him good-bye on his deathbed. My God, what have I done, dearest daughter?

It was her body that woke her when it sensed that Dashing Douglas Fairbanks Rodriguez was no longer there in the brass bed. It was not quite light outside yet, though there would be buses on the road at that hour, and he would have flagged one down to get back into Asunción in time for a new day. At thirty-five it was still an easy thing, a reflex, to wake into expectation. She wondered whether she was surprised that he was gone. It didn't matter.

She lay there as the light gathered, a tawny cat with a torn ear nesting in the covers at her feet, and listened to the voices. *Gracias a Dios* they were back. They were a mystery, and the profoundest pleasure. A person could live without many things—her own fifty-five years proved that, over and again—but not without those. She had to have the voices, had to hear them running like water in an underground cave in a country to find which there was no map. No end to the voices because no beginning.

When they faded she felt serene. She had no urge to get out of bed. The day was going to be intolerably hot, murderously hot. It was the heat, and what it stood for, that killed her parents. She thought of Katrina du Champs in her Cologne years, years of shimmering promise that required not so much success as simple hope to be the perfect halcyon they were. After the nasty incident with the barrel-maker's son she had written up a storm. Her father, eager to reap the profits from his investment, watched in amazement as she sat at the piano hour after hour, day after day, furiously scribbling score upon score on the special paper that he himself went out to buy with the dregs of his inadequate inheritance. He had received a letter from an acquaintance in Alsace describing a property up for sale that was so exactly what he wanted in a country home that it would be a tragedy to let it pass into anyone else's hands. Write, my dear daughter, write, he whispered to her every time he bent to kiss her perspiring forehead. She wrote.

The melody was there before the words, but the words were not long in following. Katrina Webern captured both of them before she got out of bed. They came the way her better pieces always came, engraved so deeply in her brain that she could put off committing the music to paper for a couple of hours while she breakfasted and fed her prowling beasts. She would devote those two hours to coming up with the right name for the song, which was in some respects a departure, unlike any of her previous efforts. The certainty of how new, and how good, the music was encouraged her in a physical way. She felt energetic and capable and unaccountably fortunate. The difference between making up and making over was, it turned out, negligible. Rising, she felt equal to the task of rummaging around her house to find what it was that Dashing Douglas had taken away to pawn. The voices, Douglas be damned, were back.

the ballad
of tony nail

The day Antonio Clavo made sergeant he celebrated alone. Josefina, his wife, would not climb down from her hill of disappointment for anything less than a major, and Clavo knew he had risen as high as he was going to rise in the Honduran army. There was no middle ground for the two of them to stand on. Anyway he had been plagued all day by a roaring in his head, wind down a tunnel, that left him too irritated to be sociable with anybody. In late afternoon he found a bar with no television in downtown Tegucigalpa and parked his body in the least uncomfortable chair. He drank beer slowly and shelled hard-boiled eggs, which he rolled in a powder of salt and pepper and swallowed whole. He was twenty-seven years old, and he wondered how long he could stand being alone.

Clavo loved Tegucigalpa. Everything about the city suggested security to him, and stability: The way pockets of sun-warmed air got trapped in alleys on cool evenings, the way you could walk and smell tortillas cooking on some stranger's grate, and then the sound of mariachis practicing would come at you from an unexpected angle like a friendly ambush. The way you would crest a rise sometimes and see red-roofed houses folded into the clefts of green hills, civilization sustained in grace by the laws of physics. Even the way the ground swelled up to embrace buckled concrete and crumbling bricks seemed to reassure you that the earth underneath the city was a place that protected you, held you up.

That was the problem with drinking alone; you were likely to float away on your own private wave of sentimentality and no one around to throw you a life preserver.

He had seen Tegucigalpa for the first time as a conscript, and he had never wanted to leave. Not that he started out with any particular affection for military life. He was fifteen and too big for his own good when a squad of recruiters pulled him off a bus in Copan. It was the smell of rum on the breath of the corporal who pinned him up against the bus that made Clavo knee the man in the groin. He took off running. He knew the lay of the land better, he thought, than any drunken dictator in a uniform and big boots. So as soon as he could he left the road, coasted light through fields of chest-high grass onto the site of the famous ruins his ancestors had left behind as testimony to their own idea of civilization.

A full moon lacquered the massive monuments of the Mayans with a pearly sheen that made him feel respectful even as he ran. People told him he looked like a genuine Indian, a purebred, not a drop of watered-down mestizo blood in his veins. One time when he was still a kid, a German scientist stopped Clavo in the road and asked to take his photograph. He told Clavo he was the pure and uncorrupted image of his Mayan forebears before Columbus came bringing disease and vice and the concept of profit to what he called the New World. The German—he was an archaeologist bewitched by Copan—burnt up a roll of twenty-four pictures of Clavo from different angles. For a few minutes of free flight, as

Clavo cut through the ruins of his people's former glory, he was the Mayan man of his own imagination, fleet and pure and noble. Then the same corporal came out from behind one of the big stone stelae and knocked him down.

No way some stranger should have been able to do that on Clavo's home ground. But looking back, he was grateful that things happened the way they did, because in ten bruising minutes he learned the nature of the world—it was hostile, and all its surprises hurt—and what you had to do to survive in it. On his back in the shadow of a noblewoman of stone, he covered his testicles with his hands and took boot kicks on his body until the corporal who had bushwhacked him grew tired of inflicting pain. Then he went quietly into the Honduran army. And never left.

Why leave? Civilian society was a fraud, it was like drawing a curtain to block out the red-fanged monster peering in through your window. By contrast, the military revealed life's truer colors. All the lessons you needed were there for the learning, and only the fools and the saints refused to profit from them. It came down to this: You did what you had to do—kiss up and kick down. You leaned hard on the ones below you, treated them mean, bullied and badgered, in order to minimize the amount of same done to you by the ones above. Simple. They told you the importance of discipline was to prepare soldiers to walk into the line of fire, but that wasn't it. Discipline was what maintained the distances between people, because sympathy could be fatal.

Never a slow learner, Clavo looked around, grasped the rules of the game, and prospered. Relatively speaking. He had gone from being the eighth son of a farmer in Copan who couldn't afford shoes to a sergeant in Tegucigalpa with a house of his own, a used Ford pickup driven down through Mexico, and his own modest share of the take in certain tax-exempt business enterprises run by his commanding officer. It would be unmilitary, and therefore dangerous, to succumb to the desperate feeling he couldn't quite tamp down that his life, at twenty-seven as a sergeant, was over. He drained his beer glass, rolled another egg in the spice powder on his plate, ordered more.

For as long as they were married Clavo had worked to educate Josefina in the same rugged school he had attended himself. But she resisted. She called him a brute who deserved the enmity of the men underneath him, who were too cowed to protest his cruelty. Too bad. Josefina was a good-looking woman, almost as tall as he and with the same trademark Mayan features, that combination of roundnesses meeting at flat angles, that he was proud to bear. Men on the street still stopped to look at her. But between Clavo and his wife something was bad. There was a hole, and the roaring sound driving him crazy blew through it relentlessly into a dark place he was afraid of.

Maybe, from the way it started, he should have known better than to expect felicity. Josefina found him on his back in a street in her *barrio* on a hill out near the airport. He was eighteen, and fierce, and combative, and lonely as the day was long. He had drunk himself into immobility; only his eyes moved, watching bright glazed stars make their slow circuit across the illegible face of Heaven.

"Get up," she told him harshly, and he got up, an accomplishment he would have thought beyond his battered body. He followed the commanding woman to a bedroom in the back of her parents' house, from which she shooed a herd of curious kids, and let her minister to his pain, which was considerable.

"Drinking is for people who can't do anything else," she told him, laying cool, capable hands on his forehead. He admired the sheen of her hair, which was the color of a crow's feather. "Not for someone like you."

How did she know he was somebody else? She knew. They got married a week later.

He should have counted the months better, but a self-preserving cautious impulse stopped him. The baby looked like Josefina, might have looked like him or not. He was glad it was a girl. The second child was a boy, and the third, and then they stopped, and

all three Clavo children grew up looking like Mayas, pure and noble. They could have been models for the stone stelae at Copan,
where Clavo took them once to stand in the bright shadow of their
recorded past.

He had to be content with just that, showing them, because they
were young, and because he never found the words to tell them
what he knew: The stone was important, he wanted them to know,
it was the symbol of civilization. It was what held you up against
the force that would otherwise suck you down. He didn't even try
to describe to his family the feeling of terror, of desolation, that had
overtaken him standing at night once in the fields on his father's
farm, when it seemed as though the earth was going to swallow
him alive, whole, and quivering. He was ten, maybe, and they had
sent him out alone on an errand of some kind. He remembered
mud, and a fecund smell of rot, and the feeling of being pulled inexorably down toward something with no bottom. But there were
neither words nor way to say that. What he said instead was *Your
ancestors knew everything there was to know about carving stone. Look at
the city they made.*

He acknowledged a degree of blame. When it was difficult to talk
he stopped trying. Then, after the hot, confusing years when the
kids were coming, even sex with Josefina became a kind of combat,
their bed a murky battleground on which the clear outlines of nothing could be perceived: not the motives with which they fought, or
the territory they contested, certainly not winner and loser. After a
while he gave up fighting, after which unreflecting decision he met
every advance she made with the invincible weapon of indifference.

It was not good to think in a straight line about Josefina; experience had taught him that. Without tasting it he finished his last
beer, left the last egg unshelled, and went out to walk in the city of
his dreams. The beer had bloated him; along with the roaring
sound the result was a discomfort that induced anger. In the pleasantly cool night air of early spring Tegucigalpa was red.

An unfamiliar music drew him off the street into the municipal theater. He liked it that no one at the door challenged him for a ticket he would not have bought. Service to his country brought small recompense, so it was important to take what was offered. He took a seat in the middle of the darkened theater and watched an outrageous performance acted out on stage. He must have come in somewhere past the middle of the piece, because the performers had already reached a disturbing level of intensity. A dozen or so men in black leotards, their faces painted with bright colors into twisted, exaggerated expressions of fear, and anger, and delight, danced to a music Clavo would have said was classical except that it was terribly strident, an aggressive kind of music you wouldn't choose to listen to for its own sake.

Actually the music was perfect for the dance, which was like nothing he had ever seen or imagined in his life. The dancers moved together, copying each other's moves in perfect, slinky synch, but what was it they were doing? Their ridiculous gestures, and posture, their ridiculous rolling and mocking and sweeping movements suggested everything and nothing at the same time. Were they supposed to be hunting, or fighting, or worshipping, or celebrating something? Impossible to say. He watched a prematurely bald man with a painted expression of glee lean over a thin boy whose mouth was a giant white O, and as the music crashed and banged through the theater's scratchy sound system the two of them seemed locked into a moment of their own that was both private and public, saying or doing something to each other that made the roar in Clavo's head increase in intensity until he thought he might black out. He gripped the sides of his seat in a fury of anger, closed his eyes until a wave of nausea passed. When he opened them again the stage was empty except for the same offending pair of men, frozen in their moment of strained intimacy, and the music drained away into the dark.

There wasn't much of a crowd, but the hundred or so people in the theater responded with mystifying enthusiasm to the performance, which already seemed like a dream to Clavo, something you weren't sure had really happened. These people knew something he didn't want to know, found their ugly secret confirmed for them in the dancers' performance. Seeing that made Clavo feel more absolutely alone than he had felt in the bar. The lights went out, then came back on to light an empty stage across which two bats flittered and swooped in unconscious imitation of the dancers. Then the dancers themselves, painted faces flushed, chests heaving with exertion and triumph, came back to take their drawn-out bows. Strangest of all, Clavo noticed his own hands clapping. He stilled them immediately. Never in his life had his head roared with such intensity.

He sat waiting until the theater emptied. Then, ignoring the curious usher who wanted to go home but wondered what a grunt like Clavo was doing in a place like this one, he found his way back behind the row of private box seats on the first level to the curtained stage.

What he saw there was as strange and unenvisioned as the performance itself had been. Moving in shifting circles, the dancers were hugging one another, in groups of twos and threes and fours embracing, rubbing sweaty backs and shoulders, smearing the paint on each other's faces in a kind of postperformance euphoria that touched Clavo in a deep spot inside he hadn't known existed. Part of it was the beer, and the blasted roaring, but he was suddenly weak with unwanted new knowledge of a part of life he had not been able to conceive of. Too much, too fast. He couldn't take it all in. His ignorance humbled him, shocked him, made him still angrier. His legs came close to buckling.

Then they were aware of him. All of them at once, as though he had suddenly materialized for their benefit as a kind of dark counterweight to their ecstatic lightness. A woman in a white dress with red-black lipstick nestling a bouquet of roses against her bulging breast opened her mouth as if to scream, but it was a man's dramatic falsetto that filled the space she opened. "It's the Armed Forces, *chicos*. Saved at last!"

He knew they hated him. That much at least was predictable. They hissed at him, taunted him, told him to go away to a place in Hell where he and his miserable kind were wanted. But they didn't really mean that; he could tell they liked having him there. He was the perfect foil, the perfect target for their semihysterical outrage and abuse. Their hate made him strong.

What was dangerous was fixing on the boy, the same one who had been the target of the bald man's stylized advance on stage. He stood to one side, by himself, drying his slim, strong brown body with a towel, patting at the makeup mask that gave his face a double identity, two halves of something that didn't quite go together into one. Despite himself Clavo moved toward him until he was close enough to hear the boy tell him plainly, "Go fuck your mother, *mi general*."

Clavo couldn't tell if all the laughter was meant for him; couldn't be. There was too much wild energy, too much exuberance there backstage to be the consequence of one unexpected visitor.

"You're sick," he heard himself growl at the boy, whose eyebrows were painted in twin tapering lines. His thick black lashes, too, were heightened with something artificial so that you couldn't help noticing them when he blinked.

"You don't belong here," the boy told him. The rest of the crowd, sweaty dancers and a few tittering women in tight dresses and piled-up hair, seemed to lose interest in Clavo quickly, wrapped up in their celebration of the dance.

"What's your name?" Clavo demanded.

"I'm not sick," the boy told him, "I don't get any pleasure at all out of talking to you. Go away."

"You should be behind bars."

"I am," the boy said, "I'm a creature in your very own private zoo. You found me and put me in a cage and now you're staring in through the bars wondering what kind of animal you trapped after all. You're wondering whether the beast bites, whether it's poisonous, aren't you."

What the boy said made no sense, it made perfect sense. The roaring in Clavo's head, which he had thought could get no worse, got worse. He was twenty-seven years old, he was a sergeant, he wore big black boots. Not enough to save him from disappearing before his own eyes.

He got away, had to. He turned around, stumbling, the sound of all that laughter that might or might not have been aimed at him like a wall of sound pressing at his back. He ran in the dark behind the box seats, past the startled usher out into the lobby and then the street, where he sat on the curb and caught his breath.

When he could stand without trembling he did so, crossed the street and stood in the shadow cast by an overhanging awning on a dark brick building. He was waiting for nothing. He had no sense of time passing, but it must have, because here came the dancers in normal human clothes, their faces scrubbed clean, their bodies almost decorous, as though it were necessary to hide what they knew, the strange secrets they displayed in the dance. Clavo understood that and was sorry that he did, because it meant a level of sympathy, even complicity, he did not want to experience. For a moment he thought he would go find Josefina and buy her a bottle of Cuban rum. He had an album of Mexican *boleros* she loved; they could listen to the music and drink the rum and talk about the future of their children. One of their sons at least would be a colonel, would live on the top of Tegucigalpa way past any height scaled by his humble parents.

Certain things had to be because they did. As Clavo stood in the shadow, his body polluted by too much beer, the ragged rawness of the performance still under his skin shorting out deeply embedded circuits, the boy came out last, alone, carrying a small leather bag that must have held his costume. Did they also carry their own makeup wherever they traveled? Was there a secret guild dancers like him belonged to, a guide and protector that taught them the tricks of their perverted trade? The boy didn't walk, he lilted down the street ignoring the stares of the handful of idlers who had nothing to think about, nowhere to go except the no place they already were. After him went Clavo. He was a vacuum, a hole into which everything recognizably Clavo-like vanished except a sense of being hurt, rubbed hard the wrong way.

What if the boy got on a bus? But he didn't. Out of sight of the crowd in front of the theater the dancer walked more slowly. Clavo understood that he was relieved to be alone. Stalking behind him, he heard the boy whistle a tune that was a simplified version of the weird, grating music in the theater. Clavo followed him down tree-shadowed streets whose tangled lines of darkness were broken rarely by streetlights. Once, an invisible mariachi band behind a high stone wall struck up a favorite of Josefina's, *"El Rencór del Débil,"* and his eyes teared until they walked out of earshot of the powerful, weepy music.

They were climbing. The streets grew narrower, the cobbles rougher and uneven, the air a perceptible degree cooler. Because of the beer and the stress his body was under Clavo began to labor to catch his breath, and his irritation increased. If the roaring in his head got any worse he would have lost consciousness, but it didn't. It had reached its maximum level of expression, become a constant, so that Clavo couldn't remember what life was like without it. Eventually they reached a plaza, where the ground leveled off.

Clavo had driven past the place, which had a fine view of the city below, but for some reason had never stopped there. It was the kind of place to which fathers took their children on Sunday afternoons to run and ride bicycles and eat sweet things that caused stomachaches while their parents sat on benches figuring and refiguring the next week's inadequate budget. At night, these days, it was maybe too dangerous simply to sit; he saw only one benchful of lovers, self-absorbed with their arms around each other, their tongues tasting the salt of each other's mouths in a tentative, tender way Clavo recognized by blind instinct and wanted to praise. No. He was a sergeant, there were boots on his feet. The boots were heavy.

Running in his heavy boots, he took a diagonal walk that permitted him to get ahead of the boy at a convenient corner under the statue of a bronze soldier on horseback, some memorialized savior of the nation Clavo couldn't recognize in the darkness.

"You," the boy said. His disgust was real. No note of fear in the voice, nor should there have been.

"What's your name?" Clavo demanded again; he could not begin to understand what was happening to him without knowing the boy's name.

"If I tell you my name will you go away?"

"Say it," Clavo threatened, proud that he was still in shape enough to muster an impressive level of threat, and mean it.

"My name is Dionisio," the boy acquiesced. "Now can I go?"

"Who are you?" What kind of question was that?

"Who am I?" the boy echoed him. He thought that one over a few moments before telling Clavo, "I'm what you need, I'm what you're not. Fair enough?" Then he turned and would have walked away, but Clavo caught him by the arm, bent the arm behind his back, held on hard. He derived no pleasure from inflicting that small amount of pain.

"Let me go, please. I know you can hurt me. You don't need to prove that to either of us."

"Have you done your military service yet, or did you buy your way out?"

That made the boy laugh. "I've done my duty to my country. What is it you want from me?"

There was just enough yellow light from a bulb fastened high to a tree down the path that Clavo could make out the trace of makeup on the boy's face. The shadow of an exaggerated O around the mouth infuriated him. Without wanting to he slapped the boy in the face hard with the heel of his free hand.

The boy flinched, cried a little from the pain, tried to pull away but knew he could not. "It drives you crazy, doesn't it? Wanting what you can't have, I mean. I'm what you need, *mi sargento*, I'm what you always wanted."

"Who are you?" Clavo shook him.

The boy straightened up, suddenly strong and resolved, as though answering the question clarified something he himself had been wondering about as well. "I'm the love you'll never know," he told Clavo calmly.

There was only one thing to do. Clavo did it. Winding up his full strength he knocked the boy down, kicked him hard, watched him go. Out. The eyes closed, and Clavo knew he would be in no position to answer necessary questions. That was all as it had to be.

What was new was just as necessary. The lovers on the bench behind them neither knew nor cared what might be happening outside the perimeter of their passion. Clavo dragged the boy off the concrete path onto the grass below a bunch of trees with low, drooping branches. For some reason it was like going into his father's muddy dark fields at night when he was ten and susceptible to annihilation, except there was a sweetness in the smell of grass and growing. His body craved the security of a stone city around him. For a moment he closed his eyes, worried about the line of blood that began seeping from the boy's mouth when he moved him.

Then he found himself on the ground next to the boy he had assaulted, cradling him in his capable arms as he felt to discover a pulse. There. But the boy slept, temporarily anyway out of his misery. Clavo felt generous; it was he who had given the boy such ease. He knew there would never be words to describe what it felt like to kiss that irritating mouth, smoothing it into acceptance, to hug those bony shoulders. He felt a great peace, a burden being lifted, and realized the roaring was gone from his head. In its place came its opposite, a perfect, clear quiet worth any sacrifice, any imaginable cost. In its place appeared, like a vision, the love he would never know.

His fingers found Dionisio's windpipe and pinched, a little. What happened next was still to be discovered. It mattered. But what mattered more, to Clavo's way of thinking, was what he heard in the soothing quiet around him, inside his head. There it went, and he heard it, the unstoppable going of a love he would never know. It went, and Sergeant Antonio Clavo kissed it away.

solidarity in green

When Michael Mal-
lory planned their trip to Honduras, getting his brand-new stepson
kidnapped by panhandling guerrillas did not figure in his calcula-
tions. In the years that followed Mallory's Peace Corps tour, the
dirt-poor little country had grown greener in his recollection, hallowed by its unequal struggle. The hills he remembered hiking
were inhabited by forbearing, folk-wise farmers who wore their
yoke of poverty with muscular grace. In the north coast valleys, expatriate overlords made sure that brown backs stayed bent through
generations of the production cycle that put world-class bananas on
gringo breakfast tables for pennies. Then in the eighties came the
Contra, like one big mercenary turd shat from the bowels of the
Reagan Administration to befoul the pleasant, put-upon land. Even
then, under that load of waste, Honduras kept smiling green. Then

in Tegucigalpa Derrick took a walk around the block and didn't come back.

You couldn't blame Rebecca for freezing up. Back in Nebraska, Mallory had built up for her an ideal Honduras, a magical place of green innocence. They had been married just eight months. They dragged along her fifteen-year-old son, so you couldn't call it a honeymoon postponed. But Rebecca was eager to see for herself the place where Mallory had lived his own personal golden age. Then what she saw made her freeze.

At first they both figured Derrick was staying away just to dramatize his discontent. Though Rebecca had divorced when the boy was a baby he had grown up wounded by the absence of a father, and Michael Mallory was more trespasser than substitute. Derrick knew how to sulk. Bony-thin and too tall for his body, he sweated in the Honduran heat and grew pimples that were like the greasy badges of his suffering. The boy had invented his own mythical past: Inside his expensive headphones the Fugs, the Troggs, and the Mothers of Invention replayed revolutionary music that might still change the world. How many fifteen-year-olds across the USA had even heard of the Velvet Underground? The music, Derrick had let Mallory know once in a conversation occluded with metaphors as dense as lead, was the only message. It was his identity, which quivered like light. He disappeared without taking his Walkman, which should have made them suspicious right away.

When Lenín Ramirez came to the hotel to deliver the message with the guerrillas' demands, Mallory realized the mistake he had made. In the course of the interview for Radio Testigo—the human-rights activist's shield and cause and life's project—Mallory had mentioned casually that he was enjoying staying at the Quixote, the same low-budget hotel he had stayed in as a volunteer years before.

"They're desperate, Miguelito," Ramirez explained. They were speaking in Spanish in the cafeteria at the Quixote, which kept Rebecca out of the conversation, giving Mallory time to think how he would tell her. "They are desperate because they are flat broke. It's the first time they have done anything that involved a child."

Lenín Ramirez was an engine, a force of nature, a wind that blew down trees. Something like six-foot-five, as flat and muscular in full middle age as he was in 1967 in Bolivia with Che Guevara, the man still exploded when the wire of his righteous indignation was tripped. A teetotaling ascetic, he had taken on a generation of military antagonists for whom the defense of civil liberties equaled the appeasement of world communism. The story went that Ramirez, a revolutionary at eighteen, only missed getting blown away with Che when a Bolivian contact forgot to pass him a message about where to meet. When he returned to Honduras in the mid-seventies, Radio Testigo became the vehicle his big V-8 engine of outrage powered.

Once when he was a volunteer in Santa Barbara, Mallory had seen men in uniform drive off in a truck with a *campesino* farmer known for his loud-mouthed rhetoric on land reform, which had become bogged down in a bureaucracy of vested interests. He contacted Lenín Ramirez to denounce the abduction, and something like a friendship developed. Ramirez had been the one Honduran to whom Mallory wrote consistently in the intervening years, sending him, when he could, a small solidarity check for the radio. It had been the most logical thing in the world for Ramirez to interview Mallory. The American had kept up his Spanish. And he experienced a gratifying sense of connection describing his research on land-tenure patterns in the Andes to Hondurans of good faith tuned in to Witness Radio. It was in the chatty moments after the interview proper that he mentioned staying at the Quixote.

"Tell him Derrick can't speak a word of Spanish," Rebecca asked Mallory. She sat by his side in a cafeteria booth of peeled red leather, rigid with her premonitions. Hands clasped resolutely around a sugar bowl, Ramirez faced them both in an attitude of pained calm. Even under stress Rebecca was collected, attractive in a way that made Mallory marvel at his luck. She never seemed to sweat.

Compact, pale-complexioned, she looked like what she was: the young college professor every male student dreamed of conquering. Her layered black hair had its own style, one Mallory had never seen on anyone else. Her light white dress was the perfect thing for Central America. The enormity of his guilt overwhelmed him.

"They must have been surveilling you, and they saw that the boy was with you," Lenín thought aloud, looking into Rebecca's face as he spoke. She nodded gravely before Mallory translated.

"Tell him we will cooperate entirely with the people who have Derrick," Rebecca told her husband, addressing Ramirez. Mallory heard her exhale quietly, letting the air go guardedly, a distress signal only he could detect. He translated. Lenín nodded respectfully, as though a studied civility was just the thing to keep them all from frantic panic.

"The thing is this," the human-rights activist explained. "They want half a million dollars."

"That's absurd," Mallory protested. "We're college professors. We don't have that kind of money, Lenín. You know we don't."

"What's he saying, Michael?"

"The other thing they said was not to get in touch with the Honduran police, or the American Embassy."

"Did they threaten?"

"Please, Michael, I need to know what Lenín is saying."

"If you contact either, they said, they will kill the boy."

"Of course we won't contact them," Rebecca said when she heard. The message they agreed to send back through Lenín was a promise not to go to the police, and to wire down as much money as they could come up with. Ramirez agreed that a good-faith attempt to cooperate would buy some time. Mallory made the necessary calls back to the States from their room. Then he and Rebecca stripped and lay on their backs in bed under a grating ceiling fan that cooled the sweat on their skin teasingly. Mallory explained how the guerrillas had learned where to surveil.

"It's not your fault," Rebecca reassured him. He listened for the echoes in her voice that would tell the truth, that all of it was his fault, that he had brought them to a Honduras he had never known or dreamed, but all he heard was the controlled terror for which, he knew, he was entirely responsible.

"I think we ought to call the embassy," Mallory told her. "This is their job, this is what they're here for."

"What if the guerrillas have our telephone tapped? Then they will kill Derrick." She shook her head back and forth on her pillow emphatically.

"They don't have the technology to tap phones, Rebecca."

"How do you know that, Michael? Can you guarantee me the phone isn't tapped?"

Perversely, the combination of her helplessness and his guilt aroused him, but he was afraid to touch her, no matter how tentatively. Having lost Derrick, he had forfeited any privilege of consolation. For a moment she stared at his erection but said nothing. In the stagnant heat he quickly wilted. Instead, Mallory tried to put in unalarming order for Rebecca some of what Lenín had given him when she left them alone a few minutes. Derrick was being held by a small group of guerrillas who had splintered in the eighties from the revolutionary shaft. The Unified Revolutionary Strike Force (FAUR) was ideologically unbending, rhetorically shrill, and uncompromising in its indictment of global imperialism. Through the wavy glass of their political prism even Ramirez came out looking like a bourgeois collaborator; they condescended to talk to him only to oblige him to pass their ransom note to Mallory.

Because it came down to that: money. When the Eastern Bloc empire went belly up the money that had kept the FAUR tenuously alive dried to a trickle and then evaporated altogether. A campaign of fund-raising expeditions to antiimperialist governments netted them zip. Then a bank robbery they planned went bad; perhaps they had been infiltrated by military intelligence. In any event the police ambushed and executed every mother's son in the sizable squad sent to knock over a bank chosen carefully for its provocative imperialist affiliation. The FAUR was demoralized. Then an enterprising *militante* caught Mallory's radio interview and came up with a practical plan to get some quick cash.

While they waited, Mallory watched Rebecca ice. It was not quite like denial; the fear was too fresh, too raw. More like a strategic retreat into a cave from inside which she could keep her eye on the entrance, keeping danger out. He wanted to get through to her but realized just how new they still were to one another. Eight months was nothing.

The morning after Derrick disappeared, Mallory and Rebecca sent word through Ramirez that they had ten thousand dollars in cash to trade for the boy, no questions asked. It took just two hours for their offer to be turned down. Ramirez came to their room dour and tense and, Mallory saw, profoundly embarrassed for what the FAUR was doing.

"I tried to make them understand that you are not rich people," he apologized, "but they seem to have lost the ability to reason. Or that is their pose, I don't know. Perhaps you should get in touch with your embassy after all."

"No," Rebecca snapped reflexively from the mouth of her cold cave.

"Tell them," Mallory said slowly, his emotions flattening out as he spoke into an imitation of calm, "that I will make a trade."

"What trade, Miguelito?"

"Me for Derrick."

Mallory could not interpret the little noise Rebecca made; it was not quite a word.

"They might buy that," Ramirez nodded, squaring his shoulders as if the idea really meant a happy way out. "It would be more respectable for them to hold an adult."

The wait for Ramirez to return with the guerrillas' answer was intolerable. June was high rainy season. At about dusk the city bowed its head and took on the shoulders a rainstorm that fell like an undeserved beating for a full hour.

"All my thoughts are small and simple," Rebecca said once when the rain ebbed. Absently she had picked up a textbook, though she did not open it. Mallory understood the impulse to find and perform something familiar. Rebecca reached for what she knew. She was, above all things, a teacher. Her thesis on comparative cartography had been published, then gone to paperback. *Maps and Empire* got Rebecca early tenure and the academic momentum for her pet project, the development of a globe that put the Northern Hemisphere on the bottom. The point, she believed, was best made visually. "I want him back, and I'm afraid, and I feel very small. That's the size of the universe now."

"I'm going to make an effort to get through to Derrick," Mallory told her. "When this is all over, I mean. I just need to come up with a new way to try."

She nodded as if what he had said were the reasoned conclusion to a conversation in which both had communicated expertly, clear as church bells.

At midnight when he explained the counteroffer Ramirez was careful to offer no advice. The guerrillas would turn over the boy in exchange for Mallory and the ten thousand dollars.

"If they have you, but they think they cannot get any more money out of us, they might be tempted to kill you," Rebecca thought aloud. Ramirez understood enough English to nod.

"What options do we have?" Having constantly to translate permitted Mallory to feel temporarily removed from the problem of getting Derrick back. He felt no stir of selflessness or courage, just a nagging dull desire to know nothing, to be past the nightmare.

Rebecca sat straight-backed on the bed, Mallory and Ramirez in rickety-legged chairs on either side of her. The big Honduran folded his arms violently across his chest and slumped.

"You could still try your embassy," he offered.

But Rebecca shook her head stiffly even before the translation. "Tell them we accept," Mallory said in Spanish, "but we have to agree on how to make the trade. I have to know Derrick is free."

"It's set up, Miguelito."

"Meaning you knew I was going to accept their offer . . ." Had that been strictly loyal on Lenín's part? Mallory felt his ability to judge impaired; he wasn't thinking in a straight line. Ramirez shrugged to remind him they had no options.

The FAUR insisted the trade be made at night, which meant another full day of waiting. Rebecca tried to stay close, but talking didn't work. Mallory could not abide her hope. She wanted to make love, but the most he could manage was to smother a self-indulgent comment about fucking a corpse. At nightfall he asked her not to go down with him to the grimy lobby where Ramirez waited.

"There's no conceivable gain for them to kill me, Rebecca. From their point of view all that will do is bring down the wrath of the CIA on them."

She kissed him like Hollywood; all the way down the gritty tiled stairs he sloshed the taste of her saliva around in his mouth. Everything bad that happened or that might still happen, he told himself, was one-hundred percent his fault.

Ramirez's car was suitably anonymous, a beat-up Toyota compact that looked like five thousand others on the streets. The founder of Radio Testigo drove sloppily as a *taxista* away from the grid of colonial-era streets toward Colonia Kennedy, the kind of sprawling, headless neighborhood in which anyone who tried could become invisible.

"It's simple," Ramirez explained as they went. "You walk in, Derrick walks out and gets in the car. I turn over the money to them after Derrick is back in the hotel."

"And they bought that? They're not afraid we'll set them up?"

"They bought an insurance policy."

"You . . ."

"Supposedly one of the *muchachos* is standing by at the radio with explosives. If the exchange falls apart he blows the station."

"And everyone will blame the military. Cute, Lenín. They're bastards, aren't they?"

"Listen, Miguel. I will do what I can to lobby for you. There may be elements in the FAUR who are not quite irrational."

On a street Mallory knew he couldn't find a second time Ramirez parked in front of a pleasant stucco house fronted by unkempt flowering bushes whose branches cast exquisite trembling shadows in the soft-edged white light from a streetlight on the corner. Somewhere down the street a Mexican *ranchera* played plaintively: *¿De que Manera te Olvido?* It was a night that called for a moon, but none to be had. After just a few minutes a light in the front window of the pleasant house went on, then off again.

"That's it," Ramirez told him. "Go on in. Don't worry. They need the money so bad they'll be happy to let Derrick go."

Mallory realized then the absolute poverty of his imagination. He hadn't known just how scared he would feel, how difficult it would be to walk in and surrender himself to hungry, radicalized guerrillas for whom the United States was the source of all evil in a miserable world. Later he wished he had been able to come up with a dignified way to part from Ramirez, some sane and pithy coda to illuminate the moment, which might have had its music. As it was he simply walked toward the little house like a man who might change his mind.

Inside the unlit foyer he was grasped, grabbed, a sweaty hand held over his mouth. He gagged, then followed whoever led into a back room that might have been a kitchen. Surrounded by men who looked like taxi drivers or lottery ticket salesmen or out-of-work housepainters, Derrick sat at the table sullen as ever, hands bound for symbolic effect. Seeing Mallory was like revelation. Mallory figured no one had spoken enough English even to let the boy know that his release was being negotiated.

"Michael!" His voice cracked like a choirboy's, and Mallory saw something fine and alive in his face, a new intelligence, that his conditioned sulk could not conceal. Being kidnapped had done something good for Derrick, who would walk out with a story at least, and—better still—a new perspective from which to meditate on the

Fugs' version of revolution. One of the lottery ticket salesmen untied the boy's hands while the rest watched, wooden conspirators in a dull plot.

"There's a Toyota parked in front of the house, Derrick. The man inside is named Lenín Ramirez. Lenín's a friend. He'll drive you back to your mother at the hotel. It's okay."

"What about you, Michael?" Mallory was pleased as a father at the boy's brash new intelligence. He had figured out the deal.

"I'll join you later. I have some details to work out with these people."

Derrick was permitted to stand. He nodded soberly, chafing his hands, and Mallory saw that he might in fact have come to appreciate Rebecca's son. Over time. He, too, had once thought that blows against the empire would bring it down.

Their English was like a shield, but its magic was only temporary. Derrick was pushed out of the lit kitchen, down the dark hall, and Mallory heard the door open then close again quietly, a domestic sound that reminded Mallory he was not at home.

None of his captors wanted to talk. They gestured for Mallory to sit in Derrick's chair. He sat. Stupid to resist as they bound his hands, his feet, and put a soiled gag in his mouth. Someone knocked him on the head once but he was conscious when they put a burlap bag over his head and lifted him like soft-sided luggage. Did air penetrate burlap? It must. The fear was still there but dissipated, as though some noxious substance were invading the innocent cells of his abused body. But there was room as well for a kind of rocking lassitude, a passivity he could almost enjoy. When they carried him outside he knew it was the trunk of a car into which they dumped him. Inside he smelled oil and gas, grease and rubber, and something rank like the carcass of a dead animal. He knew before the engine turned over that they were going to leave the city. He knew, when they did talk, that they would not be discussing land-tenure patterns in the Andes. He knew there was no more idyll.

* * *

Mallory figured 007 was due to show up from the vehemence with which Comandante Flechita slashed his stick at the high grass on the margin of the yard. The menace that 007 tossed off went in all directions, could land anywhere, even on the blameless *muchacho* assigned to guard the golden gringo. At the conclusion of the rebel leader's first visit to the hideout Mallory had observed 007 smack the younger man's face with the flat of one horny hand hard enough to humiliate. That's for nothin'; now go do somethin'.

"You going to let him hit you this time?" Mallory called from the yard in front of the mud-wall shack to which the guerrillas had marched him the week before.

For a moment Flechita stopped slashing, looked at Mallory captive and thought about smiling. Decided he would not. Flechita was squat, pale-skinned as a Spanish princess but with the face of an adolescent rhinoceros, minus the horn. His eyes were always disappearing in pouchy slabs of skin. He had grown up on the north coast on one of the banana plantations. The company-funded school taught him how to read, but his first lover's brother—a political scientist who had studied in Mexico—taught him what. Flechita was serious and smart. What he read in the big book of injustice led him inexorably into action. Which didn't mean he had to like getting knocked around by 007. He bent his broad rhino face and attacked the wet grass again.

Past the grass where Flechita flailed, the stony ground sloped away in pine woods that grew denser in the distance, hiding the view of saber-toothed rainy-season clouds filing the tops of green mountains that Mallory knew must be there. The FAUR knew how to pick a hideout. In a week not a single errant *campesino* had wandered past the camp, to which no trail led. Just Mallory and his guard Flechita. Just storm wind impaling itself on pine-tree spikes, and the musical angst of nervous birds, and the secret slitherings of animals that would never let themselves be seen and shot. Mallory had plenty of time to look around and absorb the anonymous acre in Honduras on which his life had been cut in half, plenty of time to think of all the things he might never be able to say to Rebecca. He had been robbed; he was angry.

Despite the bond between captor and *capturado*, despite the unending hours of politically intimate conversation that Mallory nurtured, Flechita was careful not to untie the ropes binding the gringo's hands and feet unless the Honduran had a gun trained on him. Urinating under the scrutiny of a semiautomatic rifle continued to distress Mallory; he felt defiled. Important not to let predictable emotional reactions get in the way of his plan. Turning Flechita was his only option. He waited for the Honduran to thrash away his own case of jumpy nerves.

Lunch was breakfast was dinner. Tortillas and beans and every other day some gristly beef. Flechita loosened the rope on Mallory's hands and they ate companionably in the yard listening to the wind express itself. Mallory folded a tortilla around a hunk of mashed beans that needed salt; his mouth watered of its own volition. "I just want to get your logic down straight, Flechita. If I'm going to die you owe me that much."

"Who said you're going to die?" The Honduran chewed as though his food were sour and he could scarcely keep it down.

"Do me the courtesy of not lying, anyway. It's bad manners to lie to a condemned man. In my country before they execute you they give you a cheeseburger, some french fries, and a chocolate milkshake. It's the law."

"Here it's just beans." The disappearing eyes smiled slyly.

"So the logic of the FAUR is, you are holding me personally responsible for the sins of the banana companies in the bad old days."

Flechita shook his head ponderously to disagree. "The FAUR needs money to keep going. We can't let money be the reason we give up the struggle. You represent money."

"And if my people can't come up with any? My father drove a

taxi, and he's dead. My mother washed dishes in a nursing home. Where's the money?"

Flechita looked behind him as if to spy out the money; what he was looking for, Mallory realized late, was 007. Better not to be surprised talking intimately with the gringo. A few nuggets of cold rain thunked, and Mallory shivered.

"What I really want to know, Flechita, is whether you as a person, apart from the FAUR, can accept the idea of killing me."

"There's such a thing as discipline, Mallory."

"Yes, and such a thing as individual conscience, as making up your own mind."

Mallory knew he had hit home; there was a chink there to be hacked at. What he needed was time to hack, but 007 when he came left him thinking there would be too little to accomplish anything.

Handsome as a poet, with gray eyes that ambushed and a supershort gray beard, 007 might have been fifty. He had been one of the principal renegades who founded the FAUR. There was no road to the hideout; he and three housepainters with expensive rifles and cheap machetes came walking up through the damp woods like tourists who had lost their way. Head down, Flechita heated coffee on the small fire he stirred.

"Ramirez says your people are unable to raise more money," the guerilla leader told Mallory. "Maybe they don't love you."

"Not all gringos are rich. You must have known that."

When 007 shrugged, Mallory wondered how far the man could be pushed before he blew up and smacked him. He assumed the FAUR's James Bond was, after all, licensed by somebody to kill. "There is one other option. We are informing the American Embassy that we have you, and that we will turn you over for two hundred thousand dollars."

"The embassy won't deal. It's government policy."

"They dealt with Iran and the Ayatollah."

"That was a mistake."

"The hypocrisy of the American government exceeds belief.

They'll pay. Your congressman will write to the president. They'll show your picture on television. You can go home and write a book and get rich."

"It won't work." Why was it so important to keep on making the point, when making it might get him killed? Mallory had a bad moment when he thought that one of the other FAUR *militantes* was going to trade places with Flechita. But 007 walked abruptly away escorted by the same contingent he came with. The guerrilla leader appeared relaxed and hopeful, as if he was sure the U.S. government would cough up some spare change for the life of a taxpayer. He left without hitting Flechita, who celebrated by letting Mallory go for a walk in the woods, hands tied behind his back. The guard trailed behind with his gun, safety off.

That night, passively letting himself be trussed on his shuck mattress like a chicken going to market, Mallory asked Flechita, "You know my government isn't going to pay a nickel to free me, don't you?"

Flechita straightened the rope tight around Mallory's feet and nodded. "I know they won't."

"Does the idea of my getting killed, when 007 figures that out, bother you?"

"There's such a thing . . ." Flechita began, warding him off, but he did not complete the sentence. He blew out the lone candle that lit their shack and fell heavily onto his own shuck mattress.

Mallory had been sleeping deeply and easily in the shack despite being tied, as if constraint was a good thing. He lay listening to Flechita lapse into belchlike snoring, then drifted himself into a place thick with dream, the images clots in a sluggish river of dumb thought.

The rain that had been hoarded all day woke him when it finally came. Flechita was breathing more quietly, hard to hear over the wet wind in the rain-battered woods. Lying listening, Mallory tried to visualize Rebecca's face, her body, to conjure up her smell, but all he could grab was an opaque fantasy. Eight months was nothing.

He felt cheated, but he was the one who had done the cheating: He had lied to Rebecca, invented a country and a state of innocence neither of which existed. It made no difference that he had believed they did. He had resisted the urge to masturbate, to get Rebecca back in that unsatisfying way.

He was suddenly dizzy. He wanted to sit up, walk around in the storm, think mobile. But his tied legs had cramped to sleep, and he felt a burning urge to urinate. Some perversion of pride kept him from waking Flechita, so he relaxed his kidneys and tried to understand what was happening to him. The main thing, he told himself as if it were a pearl of insight, was he didn't want to die.

Clutching the pearl he eventually slept. In the morning Flechita let him walk a solid hour through the sodden woods, far enough this time to see unimpeded the view of green mountains he knew must be there. Mallory's eyes were hungry. Both men watched the gray sky break up into patchy blue. Hands tied loosely, Mallory sat on an outcropping of gritty-surfaced rock. Flechita crouched a few feet away, rifle in his lap.

"I don't want to die," Mallory said.

"Maybe we're both wrong, Mallory, and your government will ransom you."

"Tell me something, *amigo*, do you really think 007 is going to let me go, even if he gets some money from somewhere?"

No comment from the FAUR.

Mallory spent the next week hacking judiciously at the chink in Flechita he was sure was there. Six days more, seven, eight. Hacking required delicacy, finesse, a sense of timing. Too much at the wrong moment, Mallory told himself, and his captor would seal up entirely. But he had nothing else to do with his time than be careful, be persistent. He was both, and he saw progress. Once, after coffee, Flechita came close to admitting that there might be a logical flaw in holding a middle-class academic as a pawn in the greater game of national liberation the FAUR was playing. What Mallory needed was more time.

The bad thing was losing track of days. When he realized he was slipping, Mallory made a pile of sticks, one for each day held. So he was pretty sure it was on the seventeenth day of his captivity that three FAUR *militantes* appeared in the woods below the shack. This time 007 did not accompany them. They called out Flechita, who came back after a half-hour swinging absently at the grass with his black-handled machete.

"Do they want you to do it yourself, Flechita?"

"Your embassy sent a message that they do not negotiate with terrorists. That made 007 furious. The FAUR rejects the concept of being lumped in with common criminals. We are revolutionary guerrillas engaged in a war of national liberation, not terrorists."

"Did they tell you to shoot me?"

"Now 007 is working through your friend Ramirez. There is one more counteroffer to be made to the gringos."

"How much time do I have to live?"

Flechita raised the machete in irritation, and Mallory thought he had made his first mistake of timing. But the rhinoceros-faced little man turned suddenly and left him. Mallory watched him pace the perimeter of the hideout yard for a long time, a parody of guard duty. The tall grass in his path suffered.

That night Mallory drilled at the guerrilla as they lay on their shuck mattresses, which had collected moisture and stank of something organic rotting. Mallory's nostrils collected dust. His nose ran as with an allergy, and his eyes burned. "I don't want to die," he reminded Flechita in the slippery dark. "It's not right, it's not correct or logical or necessary, and you know it."

"Shut up and sleep," Flechita growled at him and spat on the dirt floor.

The FAUR people had brought supplies along with their ultimatum, so in the morning there was coffee with sugar, and eggs fried in oil to go with the tortillas and beans. And salt for everything. Mallory's Pavlov tongue salivated. He could feel the grease scouring his system and was afraid he would have serious diarrhea. It occurred to him that his and Rebecca's money had paid for the food they were eating, which made it taste better. But his helplessness shamed him as though it were his fault, a grievous sort of character flaw.

"Okay," Flechita told him when they had finished washing the breakfast dishes in a plastic bucket of cold creek water. Counterproductive to play dumb.

"How do you want to do it?" Mallory said.

"It has to look like you surprised me. Otherwise they'll kill me. They're coming back for you tomorrow either way. I didn't tell you that."

"I'll leave you tied up."

"You can do that. But you'll have to hit me once, hard enough to leave a mark they'll believe."

They spent the morning discussing the details. Conspiracy heightened the sense of camaraderie that had been building, abetted by Mallory, resisted by the guerrilla. The American disciplined himself not to show his elation, not to offer any premature enthusiastic thanks.

After lunch Mallory had a hard time waiting patiently. He needed the hours of light to put some serious distance between him and the hideout. Finally he had to say it: "Flechita, can we do it now?"

The aggrieved look the guerrilla gave him distanced them from each other in an instant, giving them what they needed to keep going. They stood in the yard. The afternoon sun was cheerful, the neighborhood birds swooped and babbled brainlessly in the crisp unfiltered light. Mallory lifted his hands and Flechita untied them with exaggerated deliberation. He let Mallory free his own feet, watching him from a distance with his rifle cradled.

Free, Mallory walked haltingly around the yard a few times. "Some day when you're dying," he called to his captor, who watched him grumpily, "you'll know you did the right thing."

Their revised idea was to score the Honduran's cheek with a knife blade gently, just enough to draw some blood and leave a mark. Then Mallory would tie him comfortably on the mattress, take the rifle, and disappear. Flechita would have all night to devise a credible story. When Mallory had his legs under control he went to stand ceremonially at the doused cookfire, on the other side of which Flechita observed him with more apprehension than he thought was healthy.

Flechita handed him the knife, blade first, but when it was time to surrender his face he didn't, couldn't. "You're responsible, goddamn it," he yelled at Mallory in the voice of a man unbalanced, and Mallory wondered for what. But he knew the whole thing was quickly slipping away. No choice: He surprised the guerrilla, leaped the dead fire and bowled into him hard. They both fell, and Mallory drove his knee into Flechita's groin. The shot of pain loosened the Honduran's grip on the rifle, and Mallory yanked it from him.

The part that shaped things for Mallory was the pleasure he took in hurting the man whom he had grown to like. He had the advantage; he used it. Flechita was on his back, stunned, slow to recover. So Mallory clubbed him with the butt end of the rifle. In the chest, hard as he could bring it down. Twice. In the face, once. The Honduran lost consciousness, bled a red line from his twisted mouth. And Mallory was as happy as he remembered being in his life.

He tied the guerrilla with the same sweaty ropes that had been used on him so many times they felt like old clothes. He trussed Flechita as tightly as he had himself been trussed. But rather than drag him inside the shack to a mattress, he left him in the yard. He drank a cup of cold coffee quickly, took the rifle, and walked instinctively downhill.

He knew nobody from the FAUR was going to get him again. But he moved carefully, like one of the Honduran animals he never saw, and dropping down eventually he came to a dirt road. He tossed the rifle into some underbrush, then took the road until it dead-ended in a T at a slightly wider dirt road. It was almost dark, and he was beat, so he found a nook and slept peacefully in the uninhabited underbrush at the head of the lonesome T. He made Tegucigalpa on a misfiring recycled Bluebird school bus late the next afternoon. He was still inexcusably happy.

Walking around Tegucigalpa was like waking up after a long, dull dream of death. The noise of human traffic soothed and stimulated him. The sight of a woman in a shiny blue dress dragging a grinning child along a broken sidewalk made him want to praise and cry. The smells in the market, things frying and festering, made his mouth salivate. He went not to the Quixote but to Lenín's radio station, where the human-rights activist wrapped him in his enormous enfolding arms and roared. "Rebecca is staying with us," he told Mallory. "She sent the boy back to Nebraska. Let's go, I'll drive you home. You married yourself a good one, Miguelito. She told me she would wait for you until she saw the body. Dead or alive. You beat the FAUR, *hijo de puta*, you beat the FAUR!"

Held passive, slumped against his friend's treelike body, Mallory finally finished waking up.

★ ★ ★

In September at a Stop-N-Shop in Lincoln, Nebraska, in the bright fluorescence of plasticized plenty, Mallory began to cry. Rebecca had left him with the cart, gone around the end of the aisle to get a loaf of whole-wheat bread and some French mustard. Derrick, who had not wanted to come grocery shopping with them in the first place, watched the tears run down Mallory's face with an expression of helpless sympathy, watched his hands grip tightly the handle of the cart until the knuckles whitened. But proximity to an out-of-control adult embarrassed him, and he backed away playing nervously with the volume on his Walkman.

While Mallory cried, two or three people pushed their own carts safely past him, casual voyeurs fascinated at a display of emotion that just might be genuine, just might have reason to be. Then Rebecca was back. "I'm sorry, Michael. I'm sorry for you. I think I know, a little, what Honduras meant to you."

He shook his head. His eyes burned, his nose was congested. She took his hand and caressed it, while a bald man with a trim beard and catlike green eyes minced past them as though what they had might be contagious.

"It's not what you think, Rebecca."

"Then what is it?"

"It's Flechita."

"What about him?"

"I wanted to kill him."

She stopped rubbing his hand, and he felt her suspended next to him, listening to something he might not be able to hear himself. On a far periphery Derrick hovered fretting.

"I really wanted to kill him," he told her again. Because that's what it came down to, when it came down to anything. And it did. There was a hole inside. It would not be filled, now. "Did we get everything on the list?" he asked Rebecca. She said something that might have meant it didn't matter, and he wheeled the cart around toward the checkout counter. That was what it came down to, he was thinking. At the counter, when it was their turn, he stacked their groceries on the conveyor belt. The woman at the cash register was unusually chirpy. Out of her orange lipsticked mouth came little barks of welcome and pretended pleasure. The thing was, he remembered with fresh intensity, he had wanted to kill Flechita.

marina in the
key of blue flat

This is where they keep their soap, where they used to keep it. You hang it on the neck of the shower pipe, like this, and you put the bar of soap on the tray here, and above it you place the different bottles containing the things you use for beauty: like shampoo and other items for your hair. I did not understand the labels on the bottles, although every time I looked at them I understood something else. I understood that the people who bought those products with interesting labels did not know who I was. I do not blame them for not knowing me, but the fact remains that they did not, nor could they. Could they? Their house, which I cleaned in every corner for three years, had five bedrooms and all the bedrooms had their own showers. Every shower had one of these, and this is where they keep the soap. Where they used to keep it.

They went away, back to the United States of North America.

Although they might just as easily have come from somewhere else, like France, or Japan, and gone someplace else when they left, like Korea, or Germany. That's how they are, it's one of the differences I have observed between them and me. I have observed many differences, cleaning their houses.

Things are not good right now. My ankles are hurting. It makes me feel as though there are round caps of pain on either side, and someone is pressing the caps close against the bone.

Often when my employers leave Paraguay they give me things: Once I was given a bicycle for my son Diosnel. It was an excellent blue bicycle in perfect condition. The man, who was German, brought the bicycle to my house in his jeep, and he left in a hurry so that none of us would be embarrassed. He was a decent man.

Although it is also possible he was remembering the time I handed him a shirt that I had ironed for him and his hands came very close to touching my breasts. They may actually have touched me. I cannot say with any certainty how close his hands came. What I remember is seeing the sunlight fall in a clean, clear shaft onto the ironing board. My breasts tingled, I think, although I felt no attraction to him then or ever. I consider that he was a good man and a responsible employer. Every time he forgot to give me the supplement to pay my health insurance and I had to remind him, he pulled the money from his pocket instantly. Usually he gave me a little extra to make up for his lapse, like interest. Sometimes, if I had enough to pay my quota without asking, I let it slip for a few months. I do not remember whether I let it slip in the expectation of interest. If I did, I do not think the fault was grave.

None of the traditional songs we sing seem to have words that talk about me. They do not talk about the things I have seen, or the things that happen to me, or the powerful feelings that come to me at certain times of the day or night when I feel unprotected and hungry in a peculiar way. For that reason the traditional songs do not influence or console me as much as I wish they did.

My man Aurelio and I decided we would hide the bicycle until

Diosnel's birthday because Aurelio was not working at the time. Aurelio is not working now, as it happens, although he would like to work. I believe that he would like to work. My mother does not. The opposite things we believe about my man's interest in working have created some distance between us. Since my mother is with us in the house these days, you would think that this distance is more of a problem than it actually is. My mother's memory is no longer trustworthy, so that some of the things she accuses me of are actually events that happened with my sister, or with me when I was a child, or with her own mother when my mother was a child. Aurelio only occurs to her as a subject of complaint when he is around. It is probably just as well that he's not always around.

I was relieved and pleased that Aurelio found a job a couple months ago as a driver for the owner of a company that produces cooking oil. We celebrated. Aurelio knows how to celebrate, and he is still as attractive to me and to all women as he was when he was somewhat younger. You could see his picture in the newspaper next to an article about a famous singer or a movie star and not be surprised. Our celebration ate up a weekend and left us flat broke. We didn't care because Aurelio was working again. But last month something happened with the automobile on a Friday night that has not been completely explained to me, and once again my man is without employment.

I call it my house because the title is in my name. The title is in my name not because I distrust Aurelio, but because I considered it a prudent thing to do to put the house in my name. I hope you can see and appreciate the difference. I do not expect that he will leave me for another woman. I do not need to see in a mirror to have a realistic understanding of my own beauty.

We left Diosnel's blue bicycle with a friend of Aurelio's. The bicycle disappeared before Diosnel's birthday. For that reason it was better not to get his hopes up. Although if we had given him the bicycle before his birthday perhaps he might be riding it now.

Whenever Aurelio and I go someplace with friends—usually his friends but sometimes with people who are friends of both of us—I am asked to sing. I sing the traditional songs remarkably well. When people applaud, I know that they are praising me sincerely. Nevertheless it is no credit to me, having a good voice. I was born with the voice, which is merely a gift of God. And when I was a girl I learned the songs without even trying, the way all children pick things up without effort. What would be a credit to me is making some new songs, some songs that talk about my life, the things that I see and the things that happen to me.

I have friends who envy me, working for the foreigners in that large and beautiful house in Manorá, where all the houses are large and most of them are beautiful. The foreigners treat me better, they say, than the Paraguayans treat them. That may be true. It is almost certainly true, although I will not concede that to those friends of mine. I will not concede it because I don't think I can explain to them how working in that large house with foreign families has distressed my life. I don't think I can tell them because I don't know how to tell myself.

If I wrote a song about the things I have seen, and the things that have happened to me, I doubt they would play it on the radio, although they should. I have the voice. What I lack is the words.

This is a picture of an island in Japan. I do not remember the name of the island. It was given to me by the Japanese family when they left Paraguay. Notice the volcano, which is asleep, and the snow. I have not seen a volcano or snow. But if I had words I would write a song about an island, although not about the island in the Japanese picture. This is a knife especially made to cut bread. The North Americans gave it to me. I did not intend for the wooden handle of the knife to become bleached out the way it is. I did not know that you do not put things with wooden handles in the dishwashing machine. When I pick up the knife—in my house we cut various things with it, not just bread—I think of the look the woman gave me when she saw how bleached and sad the handle was when it came out of the machine. This is a hammer that Aurelio favors. He says he should have been a carpenter. I would have been happy to share my house with a carpenter. The French couple who had no children left this French hammer behind in the house when they left. I found it in the dirt below a bush. I have no idea how the hammer got there, below that bush. If I had taken the hammer to the French Embassy and asked them to send it to the man who had left, they would have laughed in my face. I do not want anyone to laugh in my face.

The fact that my ankles hurt when I become pregnant, as though round caps of pain were being pressed against the bones, is one of the ways in which I consider myself unique.

If I were not worried right now, I would make a list of things I would put in a song, if I ever wrote a song. Besides the island, I would put in something about a dream, because my dreams are usually interesting. I would also put in the Siamese cat that lived with the North American family, because I myself have been troubled by a feeling that was neither envy nor resentment when I saw the way those people were with that very sleek cat. It was gray, with black feet, and its eyes were cruel. I like cats, even when they are not sleek. The purpose of cats is to eat mice. I would also want to put this thing into my song, the thing where they keep their soap, except that it has no real name and even if it did you would not put the name of such a thing into a song.

This is the nature of my problem: A song that had words about an island no one has ever been to, and a *yanqui* cat, and a Paraguayan woman's dream, and a thing that hangs in a shower and holds soap, that would be a ridiculous song. Even if I wrote it, and it came out right, and I sang it perfectly, no radio would ever play it. Even though I have this problem, however, I do not think that I am a ridiculous person. I think instead that I am a person with a particular shape, and that what would make me happy is someone seeing that shape and understanding it. This is one of the ways that my life has been distressed.

It's not that I dislike the traditional songs, which talk about the beauty of our country when one is far away from it, and the sadness that often accompanies love, and the bravery of our soldiers under fire. Then what is it? It's a hole.

Last night I went to the island—the one no one has ever been to—when Aurelio and my mother got into it during our supper. If I were younger, I would have done what Diosnel did. He covered his ears with his hands and started humming very loudly. Then he ran outside and kicked at the tires of Aurelio's car. The other children followed him outside to watch. Aurelio's car no longer runs. It was already not running when someone stole the battery and the distributor cap, so the loss of those two necessary parts did not affect us the way it would have affected us if the car had been running when they were stolen. What bothers Aurelio is not knowing how or when they got at the car to steal the parts.

Since I am no longer of an age at which covering the ears is permissible, I went to the island. For that reason, I cannot say with any precision what Mother and Aurelio argued about. It doesn't matter. I think that Mother may have thought that Aurelio was my father, who left us long ago to work in Buenos Aires. We think he became a waiter there, but we are not sure. It doesn't matter. Things would be easier, it seems to me, if Aurelio were Diosnel's father. The edge between them has not gone dull yet, nor do I think it will. It doesn't matter.

It doesn't matter about my mother and my man because I recognize that what Mother is doing when she goes at Aurelio has to do with my father. Aurelio must also recognize this, and after his anger he is generally patient, or he finds something to laugh at. I remember little about my father except that the problem had to do with work. I mean the lack of work, or what it paid the man who did it. It is handy to have a man around the house but not always.

It is also possible that when the German dropped off the bicycle that did not wind up being Diosnel's birthday bike that I, too, was remembering something, and that the embarrassment my employer wanted to avoid came because he was reading my thoughts. If I am right about this, then what I was remembering and he was reading had to do with his smell, and other things. When I handed him the ironed shirt and he touched or didn't touch my breasts, which tingled or did not tingle, and the sun came in like a third person only larger and quieter, I smelled the German's cologne. He had just come out of the shower, and his body had been treated by those products in the bottles with interesting labels, and now when I think about it having that sort of shower must be like starting your life over again every time you step into the spray. If I am still right, then the smell that I recall had to do with being able to start your life over again every time you showered. I would not call that a sexual kind of attraction, or not exactly.

Things are not good, just now. There is a startling pain in my mother's chest that requires that I take her to the clinic. This pain scares both of us. However, my mother never managed to keep up with her monthly quotas, so she is not covered by insurance. The North American family has gone home. They would have given me the money I needed to take my mother to the clinic. They would have taken it out of my next month's salary.

I have been told that the owner of the house in Manorá is moving back into the place. He does not need domestic employees and would not take me if he did. If I asked, he would laugh low in his throat and tell me that I have been spoiled by too many years with the foreigners, and spoiling domestic help is what they do best.

I have a good name. It appears on the list in personnel offices at several foreign embassies in Asunción. But if there are any new people arriving, or any people already in Paraguay who want to make a change and hire new help, none of them will take me because no one will take a pregnant woman. I could lie, but the lie won't last, and then I will no longer have a good name, and it will be removed from the lists they maintain in the personnel offices of the embassies.

I would sell this bread knife for money to take my mother to the clinic, but no one will give me anything because the wooden handle is bleached ugly. Of course I would not have the knife if the handle had not been bleached. I would sell Diosnel's bicycle, but of course the bicycle disappeared before any good was gotten from it. I would sell this picture of the Japanese island, but I know no one who would pay anything at all for this sort of picture.

I would send Diosnel out to make a little cash doing something or other, but Diosnel is eleven years old, and the streets are full of boys who are eleven years old already doing the things that my boy would be able to do. Aurelio would give me the money I need to take my mother to be cared for, even though the house is my house, the title is in my name, and the mother we are talking about is my mother. However, Aurelio has no money since that unexplained incident with the automobile that belonged to the owner of the cooking oil factory. Setting that situation right cost Aurelio the money he had put aside by driving steadily for two months.

My ankles hurt like fire, although the pain is not important in itself. The pain can be tolerated. It is only important because it is the sign of my being pregnant again. I have not yet told Aurelio that we will be having another child. I have not told him because a bull-headed part of me wants him to feel only rejoicing that he will be a father again, and I am afraid the fact of our not having money or work will cause a different reaction in him. The feeling he will experience will not resemble rejoicing. What it will do is send him away. A man can always find enough money to go away on. And then it costs nothing to come home. When I say round caps I mean to suggest something that fits over the ankle bone like a shield, except that it is pain that covers the bone.

I could start with the island. For the song I am not going to write, that is. It is a green island, the shape of a diamond, in a blue sea. I can get that far even though Paraguay has no coastline, no sea of its own. On the diamond island is one house, long and low and open to the breeze, which never blows hard enough to do any damage. In the house is a Siamese cat with an agreeable personality. The cat knows its job is to catch mice, and that is what it does. At night the moon shines in the cat's eyes as it hunts, and nothing could be more beautiful if you are out taking a walk and happen to catch it. Around the island are flowering bushes of all descriptions. The bushes look like the bushes you would see anyplace else, except that underneath each one is the thing a person needs, or thinks she needs, or knows she wants, in the moment she imagines she needs or wants it. She parts the leaves and there it lies, embedded in the turned, fragrant black earth: anything she needs. If it is daytime the thing shines in the sun. If it is nighttime, the light is softer.

This morning Aurelio got up early and left the house. He said he was going to look for work. I believe him. My mother does not, but it is possible that the man my mother does not want to believe is actually my father, who may have become a waiter at a restaurant in Buenos Aires. Or not. I used to want to know the name of the restaurant, and the name of the street on which the restaurant was located, and the name of the neighborhood where you can find the street, and the postal code. It seems to me that those names and that number no longer matter.

This morning after Aurelio left the house, washed up and shaved and looking like a movie star, or a movie star's older brother, Diosnel sneaked away. Without being asked, my oldest child was probably going to look for a way to make a little money so that we can take my mother to the clinic. And buy the medicine the doctor will undoubtedly prescribe. Even though I saw him sneaking, I let Diosnel go without a word.

My mother and I agree on this: that Diosnel is an extraordinary child. Because of the pain in my ankles and my insides, I spoke sharply to the little ones when I called them to do the chores that Diosnel left undone. They looked at me with the eyes of baby birds, that bright and no understanding. The feeling I had when I saw Diosnel go, almost certainly to look for work among the other eleven-year-olds on the streets of the capital, resembled the feeling you get when a person close to you dies, and you tally the things that cannot be changed or fixed.

I knew a woman once who had no luck or money or common

sense. She walked out of her own house one morning and went to the Plaza Uruguaya downtown and tried to sell her body. But she was older than the girls who succeed at that business, and she did not know how to carry her body, and no one wanted her. After several hours she went home. Nothing about her life had improved in her absence. No one would want a pregnant woman with inflamed ankles, if it ever went as far as that. It would not.

It is possible that I was also pregnant about the same time that the German man touched or maybe did not touch my breasts. If you are already working when you become pregnant, sometimes you can continue to work. There are good Paraguayan families who will let you go on working in those circumstances. You make a deal with them, and sometimes after you deliver and rest up for a few days they allow you to bring the baby with you to their house. That works fine until the baby starts to crawl. After the baby starts to crawl you have to spend so much of your time keeping him out of trouble that the housework and the laundry start to suffer. There are only so many hours. Everyone becomes irritable at that point. The husband doesn't find the clean shirt he expected to find. The wife invites her friends to *merienda* and there is dust in places where there should not be any dust. After a while you decide to find someone in your own neighborhood you trust enough to keep your child in her house, and the tension in the house of your employers falls fast enough that you could measure the drop if you had the right kind of gauge.

Some of the foreign families will also permit you to go on working even when they know you are pregnant. The idea seems to throw them into a panic, usually. I have friends who confirm this. They begin to treat you differently, not like glass but like a bomb that might explode their house if it is not handled safely. I may have been pregnant when the German woman came into my room when I was changing to go home.

This was just before Holy Week, and I also have noticed that people pay a different kind of attention to you just before a holiday when they know that you are going to be away from them for a while. The foreigners, I am talking about. They are making guesses about your life. Although in this case it may have been just after the time I handed her husband the shirt he wanted and something happened that would embarrass and confuse us both more later than it did then, when it was not clear if anything ever happened that was anything besides the brush of hands and the smell of cologne and the possible tingle in my breasts. It is possible that the man, who was a good man and a responsible employer, said something to his wife, although I am not convinced he did.

But there she was. It was a terribly hot day, and I sweated all the way through my shower. My ankles were capped in pain the way they are now. Outside the house, in that enormous patio behind the high walls, you could hear birds on the branches of the trees, and I felt happy that the family cat—the Germans also had a cat, but it was not a Siamese, just a plain tabby—could not get at them. I was sitting on the bed bending over to tie the laces of my shoes when here comes the German wife, who was a very thin, gaunt blond woman with gray eyes the likes of which I have never seen on another person. Her Spanish was lacking. She asked if she could sit next to me on the bed.

I could not tell her no. She owned the bed the way she owned my time in her house, and even though the pain in my ankles distracted me and made it hard for me to tie my shoes, and I felt something folded in my gut as I sat there, I told her yes.

She put her hands on my face and traced the outline of my features there. "Who are you, Marina?" she asked me, but I knew she did not want or require an answer in words. I sat there waiting for her curiosity to work its way out on my face. I smelled her own washed smell, which was the female equivalent of what her husband had smelled like the day before. It may have been only one day before, but it may have been a week, or two weeks. It doesn't matter. What mattered, and I think it matters now more than then, was how the washed smell of those foreign people made me aware that she was telling me the truth with her careful hands and her clumsy Spanish, that she did not know me, the actual Marina. And couldn't. And I, the actual Marina, knew certain things I would not put into a song, not then or now.

I knew less well then what I know better, more sharply, now. For example, that the difference between them and a person like me comes poured out of a bottle with an interesting label, and I will never read those labels or feel what comes pouring out. I know that if the good German man's hands brushed the nipples of my breasts that the tingle I felt had to do with a kind of wanting that I will not call either ugly or clean, it was only what it was, a strong sensation felt across great distance. I know that it will do me no good to hate the German woman for her curious hands. For all the touching she did with them she did not feel. Nor could she.

For a woman like me, with a particular shape, what she has is what she knows. And what I know fills me up but does not make me full. I know that Aurelio went away when the sun came up because he did not want to hear that I am pregnant. And that Diosnel, whom I cherish, left after Aurelio left because he cannot abide in my house right now. He is an eleven-year-old man. I know that the pain in my mother's chest will attack both of us with the fierceness of a wild animal that hasn't eaten. And some day when it costs nothing Aurelio will come back, and my own pain in the ankles will have subsided. I know that there is money in the world, and that one way or another we will get just enough of it into our hands to keep us going.

I regret that the traditional songs of our country no longer have the power to console me. I regret still more that I will not write a new one. I might find the words to put into a new song, but I do not envision where I would put myself. The things I have seen, the things that have happened to me. When people applaud my singing I know that they are sincere. Having the voice is a gift of God. Coming up with a new song would be something else again, something better. Where in any song I wrote would I find a place to put something like this? This is where they keep the soap, where they used to keep it. Even without a song, though, I know I am the actual Marina.

mud man

I didn't want the Mud Man's eyes, because I didn't want the visions he saw with them. I knew they were both dangerous: the Mud Man and his visions, I mean. I knew, without the warning he never gave me, that his kind of clarity could hurt. I was burning garbage on the side of the road and thinking through a plan to attend the university. My older brother Alejandro had been married the week before, leaving our mother and me to fend for ourselves. My study plan was not coming together. There was something in the burning garbage that gave off a foul smell, and when the wind shifted, the smoke made my eyes tear. And then the Mud Man was there, and my real life started.

I think that where this happened matters, or it should. Picture a white mansion with turrets and black slate roofs that covers a city block, an ersatz Versailles. (A person like me is not supposed to know words like *ersatz*, but I do.) Below the mansion, a field with shaggy horses, shaggy grass so thick it will trip a person, and thin trees with the branches bunched at the top of the bole. Across the way are shacks on red dirt under mango trees. Poor people on the eking edge live in those shacks. One of them belongs to my mother.

My father went away to Argentina to work in construction, years ago. My mother believes he will come home some day. I know better. I know, for example, that loneliness in the dark is fundamentally different from daytime loneliness, and that the difference can be calibrated.

As I raked the burning pile, a motorcade roared past me. The general who lived in the mansion had been out and about. The conscript soldier on the corner of the general's block saluted as the black-windowed Mercedes went by. He was a boy of fifteen, and the rote way he lifted his hand led me to believe that he had not yet thought critically about the way our country's social system is arranged, and where he stands inside that system. Is that a provocative statement? I don't believe it is. It's the facts of things as they are that provoke. Words are just what you do with your voice, if you have one. Anyway, not long after the Mercedes dropped the general at his front door I felt someone's eyes on me, and there he was.

I don't remember when I began to think of him as the Mud Man. Not that he was muddy or dirty, but the name somehow fit him, I think because there was something of the earth about him. He made you think of things like mushrooms popping up in cow pastures after the rain stopped, and frogs banging and twanging in green swamps, and silver creeks running through black woods. Most of us have roots in the country, and we know we have given something up living here, the way we do, on the city's ragged edge.

Anyway the name came later. At the time all I saw was a striking man with ruddy, shining skin and attractive Indian features standing under a mango watching me rake. He was taller than the average person, and muscled in a lean and limber way. He was sixty, maybe, or even seventy. He was wearing faded jeans and a faded yellow T-shirt, and I remember his sandals were a little unusual, home-made from worn-out automobile tires, not something our people wear. The funny thing was the effect he had on me. From a distance he looked into my eyes, and I immediately felt a burst of enthusiasm shoot through me. For no reason whatsoever I felt jubilant, and strong, and even, though you may find this difficult to credit, something like beautiful, as though he was seeing something about me that no one else had noticed.

"Don't worry," he told me as he walked toward me. I must have been holding the rake as though to ward him off. "This isn't what you think it is."

He was wrong there, because I didn't have a clue as to what it was, or who he was, or what he wanted from me.

"I see visions. It's a gift," he told me matter-of-factly, meaning a curse.

I wish I had told him to get lost. But I didn't. I stopped working and brought him back to my mother's house as though a missing friend had turned up. My mother was out, so we sat on a bench in the back patio where I served him a glass of cool water and slices of mango, which he ate gratefully, as though he were starved.

"Watching you burn trash," he told me, "I saw doves flying in circles in the air above you."

"I didn't see them."

He shook his head. "You wouldn't. Not yet. You will, though. If not your own head, then someone else's."

Most of us speak two languages, Spanish and the tongue of our ancestors. Actually we mix the two terribly, such that our speech is a bastard; some would say an ugly bastard. It even has a name: *jhopará*. But the Mud Man spoke Guarani in its pure form. I understood him perfectly.

"Smells trigger it," the Mud Man told me. "Other things, too. But lots of times it's a smell. Like that garbage burning."

I nodded as though I understood and gave him another cup of cool water.

"Where are you going?" I asked him.

"Nowhere. The doves tipped me off. This is where I'm supposed to be, for now."

"Even if you did see some doves, they don't have anything to do with me."

"Fight it if you want. I fought it." He shook his head, but his sadness seemed like an act, part of what he had to do to trap me.

Now, distilled like this, the conversation seems strange. When it was happening, it was the most natural thing in the world. He had turned up the night before, slept under a bush in the field across the way from our settlement. When he woke it was still dark, and his body was stiff from sleeping on the ground. He sat on a mound of dirt and watched Mango Cua come awake. Before anyone stirred, he saw a pack of animals converge on the settlement and then disperse. As I understood it they were not dogs or cats or any other common beast. They were more like energy in animal form. They moved in a streaming blur, elongating over the dirt tracks that connected our homes, and then disappearing without a sound behind the shacks into the high brush.

What he said did not startle me. I felt as though he was only confirming as a disinterested eyewitness what I should have known about Mango Cua, an important basic fact that increased the powerful sensation of confidence the Mud Man generated in me from the beginning.

"What does it mean?"

"What does what mean?"

"The beasts you saw, all that energy."

"If you were smarter, you'd ask what the doves around your head meant."

"Then tell me."

He looked hungrily at the hunks of mango on the tin plate, and I gave him some more. In the house there were a few sticks of boiled manioc left from breakfast, and some peanuts, and two tomatoes. He ate all of it, and I felt privileged to be the one to feed him.

"What about the doves?" I pushed him when he seemed to have dropped the thread of our conversation.

"They're looking for a place to roost."

"In my head," I said. I wasn't sure what I meant, but he nodded vigorously, as though even if the answer were obvious it was worth recognizing.

"They light where they will, you know." It was as close as he came to a warning, or maybe it was an apology, but it wasn't anywhere near close enough.

"There's no room here for any birds," I said. Someone else, a quiet person inside me, was doing my thinking for me. Me, the normal me, I was just the lips, or the tongue, the mouth in any case out of which the sound came.

"Did you think everybody was born the same?" he asked me. "They're not."

I would have pushed him to tell me what he meant by that, but my mother came home.

Mother was happy. Old Maria Julia from the other end of the settlement had given her a handful of black tobacco cigars, the old-fashioned kind women used to smoke while they did the laundry in a creek out in the country, gossiping and wishing the men in their lives were more substantial. I did not introduce the Mud Man, nor did she register any surprise at finding him there. I watched the same effect of confidence and delight that he worked in her. She rummaged around until she found something else to feed him. He took it, ate it, then rose to leave.

"Next time, look up," he said, and I knew he meant so that I would see the doves overhead.

"What about the animals you saw, that energy?"

He shook his head. "That's a bad business. I'm getting out of it." He nodded his head several times. He was still nodding when he left our house.

"I'm going to stand by you," my mother told me afterward,

when things got complicated. "I'll stand by you no matter what." As testimonials go, it wasn't much.

When the Mud Man left, a kind of disappointment remained in the house like an afterglow. But disappointment was a generalizable emotion, applicable to other aspects of my life, and I didn't think any more about him. I spent the day looking for work downtown and not finding it. At the time, we had enough cash that I could have bought something to resell on the street: plastic cases to hold cassettes, or those lawn sprinklers in the shape of helicopters, or those soft orange cleaning cloths, or a couple of electrical extension cords. You can make a little money doing that. Intersections throughout the city are crowded with people doing it. But you have to give yourself to it, night and day, and I needed to find a job that would let me study somehow, even if it was just one course a semester. One course would keep me alive.

When I got back to Mango Cua, tired and sweaty and discouraged, the Mud Man was sitting in our patio listening to my mother tell stories about her childhood in the *campo*, and the good things that no longer existed in her life.

I sat down next to them on the wooden bench. I had one intelligent impulse to resist what was happening. "I don't want your visions," I told him straightforwardly.

He laughed gently at the notion that wanting had anything to do with it.

"You won't get mine," he told me. "You'll get your own. A little while ago, when your mother went into the house, I saw a lake of blood. Ugly beasts were swimming in it. That discouraged me."

"I should think it would," I said, angry at what he was trying to do to me.

"I'm tired of seeing these things."

"I'm sorry for you."

"I'm not asking for sympathy. I'm asking you to face up to it."

"You won't stop seeing the visions until you can give them away. That's the way it works, right?"

"Fight it, my son, if you have to fight it."

"You pay attention to what the man says," my mother encouraged me. I wished she would go away and leave us. She did not understand what was happening. Not then, not now.

"What about the lake of blood?" I asked him. I was sullen, but he didn't seem put off by my bullying.

"If a person swims in that lake, he turns into a beast."

It seemed to me, then and now, that he was talking about something political, something that had to do with the juxtaposition (there's a word you didn't expect out of me, I bet) of places like Mango Cua and places like the phony Versailles palace. It's not true, not now or ever, that I am a political agitator. That's just something that people with stunty imaginations have said about me.

"So don't swim in it," I snapped at him.

"Be respectful, *hijo*," my mother snapped.

"Might as well say don't have the visions," the Mud Man commented, shrugging with the first show of impatience I observed in him. "I'm tired of all this. I told you that before."

That night when I lay on my pallet on the floor in our house, my head was confused in a wonderful way. It was crowded with pictures, which I suppose are the intermediate stage, what a person sees before the visions start coming. I saw delicate creatures with transparent wings in the branches of our mangoes, not exactly hiding but not exactly showing themselves either. I saw a dog with human eyes and a cat with a human tongue and water flowing from a stone as though a spigot had been opened inside. I saw armies in dark uniforms face to face with armies in bright uniforms, and the faces of the soldiers on both sides were the same. And a big city riding on the back of a great tortoise swimming in an endless blue sea, and the deep striations on the turtle's back turning into legible words if you looked at them just right, and people in the city on the turtle's back screwing up their mouths to scream but without any sound coming out.

There was more, lots more.

In the morning I wanted to get downtown early. A friend who

worked there told me one of the newspapers was taking on people at their printing press. But walking to the well, which had a pump and was conveniently located in the middle of the settlement, I saw the Mud Man. He was smoking a lumpily rolled corn-husk cigarette, and he was laughing. Several local dogs stood at his heels as though waiting for orders.

"What's so funny?" I wanted to know.

"You thinking I was gone."

"Why don't you go away?"

His shrug was enigmatic. That's another word I'm not supposed to know, but I know it. I even remember the book I read it in for the first time. The book had a blue cover, and it smelled like knowledge. That's the kind of memory I have, and the kind of hunger.

"I don't want what you're trying to give me," I told him.

He ignored that. "It's not fair for one person to have to see it all."

"What about those animals you saw yesterday? What about that energy?"

He offered me a toke from his cigarette but I shook my head, and he walked with me across the settlement and down to where I could catch a number 30 bus into the city.

"This was a long time ago," he said.

"What was a long time ago?"

"I was out hunting in the woods. Down south near San Pedro, where my people are from. The woods used to be something before they cut down the trees and sold the logs to the Argentines."

"I'm not interested in the woods around San Pedro," I told him, which was a lie.

"I got twisted around somehow, and then I was plenty lost. Had to spend the night in the woods. Made myself a fire, and roasted a rabbit, and drank a little *cãna* I had with me. Fell asleep. When I woke up, there was the biggest moon in the history of Paraguay, stuck in the leaves of the trees like it wasn't ever going to climb the sky. Enough light, anyway, to see the fox on his haunches on the other side of the campfire. The fire was out, of course. You ever talk with a fox?"

I told him I hadn't.

"Took me a long time to realize that it wasn't the fox speaking Guarani to me but the other way around. I was talking fox to him just as though I'd grown up talking it."

The hard part about listening to the Mud Man, the part that made me angry, was that I could picture it happening. I did not want to be able to picture it happening, because that seemed too close to a vision, and it was no joke that I did not want to take over the visions from him. I wanted him to go away carrying them.

"The fox was going on about a little business that was happening back in the *pueblo*. Did I tell you it was San Pedro? The judge there signed the papers to give a *compadre* of his title to all the land in a village on the edge of some big woods. Families who'd lived there twenty years were being thrown off their own land."

"Your family was one of them," I said.

He nodded. He looked older than he'd looked the day before, old the way people can look after a lifetime of working in the *campo*, their bodies gradually petrifying.

"The judge's *compadre* wanted to timber the woods," I said.

"'Do something about it,' the fox told me. But what could I do? My belly was still full of rabbit meat and whiskey, and I could feel something pushing down on my heart, like a big invisible hand, and the big moon was still stuck in the black trees, and I knew there was nothing I could do. 'Be a man,' the fox said, and I knew he was threatening me. If there'd been something to do I might have done it."

"I'm tired of this story," I told the Mud Man, but he knew it was another lie.

"When the fox decided I wasn't going back to the *pueblo* to shoot the judge and his *compadre*—I wasn't going to do something he could respect—he jumped over the fire and bit my hand." The Mud Man showed me the scars, faint but visible, where the animal bit him. "Then he was gone. My hand bled for a long time. I couldn't seem to staunch it. I was worried about rabies. But it wasn't rabies he gave me."

"It was the vision faculty."

"Worse than rabies, if you stop and think about it." The idea that everything he'd seen and suffered through was worse than rabies made him laugh, for some reason. He stopped walking and laughed like an idiot until the fit went through him.

"You go on and look for work," he ordered me. When the laughter was gone, the soberness that took its place was cold, and for the first time I hated the man. Probably he also hated me. I ran to catch the 30 bus and to get away from him.

"Hey!" he called after me. "I'm not going to bite you. I don't have to."

I waited all morning to get inside the building on Benjamin Constant, but I didn't get the job, if there was one to be had. Sometimes my friend makes things up, thinking I need the encouragement. That used to make me angry until I understood why he was doing it. I guess I'm willing to forgive him for doing a stupid thing because his intentions were good.

Discouraged again, I stayed downtown until the sun went down and the heat let up a little. I spent an hour on a bench in the Plaza Uruguaya watching the whores scratch their legs and chew gum loudly because business was slow. I didn't hold their business against them, but the intimately casual way they talked among each other made me question the idea, or rather the possibility, of clean love, and that was depressing. I also spent several hours in the municipal library, where I memorized a few more words I wasn't supposed to know. I made up my mind that I would not take what the Mud Man was trying to foist off on me. There was enough to see in the world without having visions.

People in Mango Cua have been reconstructing everything that happened in a way that the police can understand. The police are helping them do that. I would like to say I forgive them, but I do not.

"I'm not going to listen to you anymore," I warned the Mud Man that evening.

We were sitting in our back patio drinking *terere*, a cool herbal tea we have that refreshes a thirsty person more than any beverage known to man. The general and his people drink it through silver straws. In Mango Cua our straws are plated with aluminum, and after a few months of use the aluminum flakes off. It bothers me to drink through a straw from which the aluminum is peeling, because I cannot help imagining that flecks of aluminum are entering my body through the tea and will eventually do it harm. That, for me, is the principal difference between the silver and the aluminum straws.

My mother drew in her breath and clucked. "The visions are from God," she insisted. "They are telling us what Heaven is going to be like when we get there. They are meant to give us the courage to keep going."

That made the Mud Man laugh, more softly than he had that morning, more human, and I marveled to see how white and perfect his teeth were. He had the mouth of a Mexican movie star. "I can't stay here forever," he said to my mother, meaning it for me.

"I don't want what you have," I said.

"I've been patient," he pointed out. "Besides, it's not something I can change, any more than you can change it. It happened."

I embarrassed my mother then by throwing my own fit. I raged, I hollered, I said cruel things to the Mud Man. I may have threatened him with a knife, although for some reason my memory is treacherous these days, and it's possible that I have invented the knife. Through the whole thing, the Mud Man sat hunkered the way you will sometimes see a *campesino* hunkered under a tree or some other handy shelter when a storm catches him out. I went to sleep angry, and when I woke in the morning he was gone.

I did my best to fight it. I filled up my time and all the thinking space I had available with getting a job. Once or twice I stole a couple of hours to read in the municipal library. They have an enormous

Spanish dictionary there on a wooden stand, and one of the things I would like to do is memorize all the words in it.

It's unfair to blame my mother for bringing on the troubles. I suppose they would have found a way to happen regardless. But I can't help resenting her enthusiasm a little.

"They want to talk to you," she advised me. "About the Mud Man."

"I don't have anything to say to them," I told her.

"I told them you'd go by Maria Julia's house later tonight."

I didn't want to go. I went. I spoke at the meeting, which went on for hours during the night out under the mangoes where there was a breeze, and people could hear the no-good son of the old man who used to fix bicycles playing his guitar off somewhere under the stars. I did not want to speak, but I spoke. I started out telling them about burning and raking garbage, and the way the smell stimu-lated the vision faculty in the Mud Man. I told them about the doves he had spotted in the air above my head, which meant that he was worn out from the visions and wanted to transfer them to me.

It would have been better to stop there. I didn't. I admit now: It felt good to let out the visions I had begun to see, and the things I thought they meant. To go from there, however, to saying that I am a political agitator is a long jump, and an unfair one. It's things as they are that provoke. I never suggested in the meeting, as they have accused me of doing, that the people of Mango Cua go to-gether and burn down the general's mansion. What would be the good of such destruction? Resources are scarce in our country. I would never advocate such waste.

In the morning the police came for me. I'm not much good in the morning anyway, and after turning in so late I was groggy. It didn't help when my mother broke down in noisy tears of supplication and fear. So my answers to their questions were not smart or satis-factory. In our language we have a word that means means spy: *pyragüe*, which means "hairy foot." The idea is that they move quietly, they're in your neighborhood, and you probably won't know which of the people who slap you on the back and shake your hand is the one who sells you out. I'd like to know which one of my settlement neighbors it was who gave my name to the police.

Because my answers were fuzzy, they took me to the police station, where they beat me up. Then they locked me up. These days when that happens the newspapers call it torture and denounce one more violation of a citizen's human rights. That makes it sound important, and it is, especially if your body is the one being violated. But what really happens has more to do with a lack of imagination on the part of policemen who don't know how to ask the right questions. Beating you up is what they know how to do. According to the story related by the *pyragüe* and confirmed by people eager to see me in trouble, I had invented the Mud Man, bringing his story to Mango Cua to stir people up. The visions were only my way of talking in code, and the purpose of the code was to communicate my plan, and the purpose of the plan was to overthrow the government. If you were a policeman and you believed that you didn't know how to ask questions very well, what would you do?

After a while they let me out, which was more of a relief to my mother than to me. Being in prison gave me time to think things through without worrying about the basics, like eating and sleeping and money. There were a few books available, and I read them all. I picked up a few new words from them, which always produces satisfaction in me. I steeled my resolve first to get a job and then to take a class at the university. And, by working slowly and patiently, I learned to live with the curse of the Mud Man's visions.

That's it. I'm still looking for work. Mother says don't worry, God will provide, which of course is beside the point but not worth going into with her. A majority of the people in the settlement shun me, and I try to guess whether they are afraid I will infect them with something powerful, or they know who it was turned me in to the police, or they are the actual spy himself. A few people work real hard to pretend nothing ever happened. Others make a big deal out of looking me up and shaking my hand. Doing that makes them feel brave, or generous, or open-minded. None of that distresses me much. Not having a job does.

The other night I was coming home late. My friend who works at *Ultima Hora* invited me to drink beer and listen to music with some other friends of his, guys from the paper who all have jobs and a little money in their pockets. They were generous in the right way, making sure I got something to eat and drink without making too much noise about it. Most of them have also been out of work at one time or another. On the way home, the general's motorcade passed me, and I ate the dust the vehicles stirred. I do not want to be like him, like any of them. Even if I did it's too late.

Then, walking in the dark by the shaggy field on the way to Mango Cua, I saw him. I mean the Mud Man. He waved. He was happy, I could tell. *Self-sufficient* is the word for what he was, and radiant. There was some kind of creature with wings in the air over his head. The wings were phosphorescent, and beads of color dripped from them onto the ground and melted, and I saw clearly enough that they meant he was free. I understood that he had come back to say thanks for relieving him of his burden. I also understood that I wouldn't see him again, which made me feel powerful and alone. It was like growing up in the space of a second, knowing that you had to live with what you had, and neither choice nor change was possible, and accepting it.

That was all. I waved, he waved once more and was gone. I went home to Mango Cua. I'm still there. Someday the visions will wear me out, and I'll have to find someone able to take them on. For now I can handle the force of seeing them, I guess. Anyway I have the sense that you can't give away the faculty until it reams you clean. Meantime people sleep, and the sound they still don't make is what makes me sad.

looking for lourdes

When an irritating blue bird with scaly orange claws landed in Xavier Murphy's hallucination he understood, for the first time in days, that he was disintegrating. Cell by cell. To stave it off he concentrated until he achieved the out-of-body experience he required. The distance helped him recall some basic facts: He was a crashed Catholic. In a rented room, in a village of fishermen on the Caribbean coast of Honduras. There was dengue fever in his body. And then the main thing: He was looking for Lourdes.

The bird disappeared. For a moment, the air in the space where it had lit sparkled as though composed of tiny whirling diamond fragments. Hallucinations, he conceded, were a by-product of disease. Visions, on the other hand, were not a product at all, they were simply vouchsafed.

The windows in Xavier's rented room were barred closed. The

ceiling fan turned jerkily, pushing the hot, stale air in a vicious circle. He had never spent time in such a place, nor had he imagined one existed.

He wanted to drift, but the man in the white suit was back. Xavier closed his eyes and visualized him: a huge, walrus-shaped individual with a pale, strained face clouded with determination. Xavier's room was on the second floor of a dry-goods store. The man in the tropical suit, which hung like a tent on his hard bulk, came up the punky wood stairs two at a time with extraordinarily soft steps: little kitty feet. In a hand the size and shape of a catcher's mitt he held a Panama hat with the band sweated through. He raised the other hand to knock. Then didn't.

Xavier knew he was standing there, stubborn as the Honduran day was long, on the other side of the door, which had no window. He listened for his breathing but couldn't catch it. The last time he showed up Xavier had caught him out. He heard the man's low, reedy rasp, which could have been the result of asthma, or emphysema, or maybe just the strain the weight put on his frame. This time, nothing.

Possibly he was a doctor. He had the look of a broken-down expatriate professional man gone to seed in the colonies, where his education and special status permitted him a certain amount of insulation from the rigors of poverty in the tropics. Xavier wanted to know something more, something specific, about what had happened in the motherland to drive him into exile with so many discomforts, so little recompense.

For as long as he could, Xavier held his breath. He didn't want the man in the suit to know he was there. Not that there was much doubt. San Cocho was smaller than a small town, and half the population had turned out to watch the gringo limp in on sore feet with an army surplus duffel bag over one shoulder. But Xavier was unwilling to give himself away. The thought of opening the door and facing down the doctor terrified him.

Eventually he exhaled.

It was ironic that the image of the doctor blotted out Lourdes so decisively. Xavier found himself having to work to bring her back: She was on the beach, in a cove east of San Cocho. The sun was going down in Easter colors: bloody purple and yellow, wound-staunching gauze. Next to her father's fishing boat hauled up on the sand, the keel still shining wet, she bent to untangle a net. She was wearing jeans and a long-tailed white shirt, untucked. Her long black hair was tied up on the top of her head. Her skin was darker than he remembered, more brown than the olive of his imagination. The way she brushed the sweat from her face, the way she bit her lip as she worked, the way her amber eyes went slightly out of focus and her breasts fell forward and her butt rode up in the air just a little, were all painfully familiar to him.

The first thing people in San Cocho told Xavier when he asked for her was that no woman named Lourdes Zarzuela had ever lived there, so it was impossible for her ever to have left and gone north to Gringolandia.

They must have been mistaken.

There was, however, a Zarzuela family. Before the dengue knocked him out Xavier looked them up. Their house was outside of town, down a hot sandy path that became the beach. All the way there Xavier's sandals crunched sea shells. Anticipation made him light-headed. The dirty-white gulls in the salt air, the sandpipers dredging and scurrying, the dry slap of the palm fronds against each other: It all stirred rich, evocative memories, which was odd since he had never been one for spending time at the beach, even when he was a kid. Big water, his instincts whispered, was not a passive danger you could fall into, it was actively malevolent.

José Maria Zarzuela looked too old to be the father of the pack of beach runts that belonged to him and his wife Daysy, who was younger and thin and suspicious. He was a silvered man, brown, wizened by work and the weather. The blood of English pirates ran diluted in his veins. He never stopped squinting, an occupational disability acquired from too many years of looking at the sun bouncing off the surface of the Mar Caribe.

Zarzuela lied.

The house, up off the beach in an ecological litter of banana trees and yucca plants and connected clusters of low-to-the-ground bushes with knives for leaves, was like permanent camping. Xavier thought the row of geraniums in rusting milk cans in front of the place was the single most effective home-improvement scheme he had ever seen. That had to be Lourdes's touch. He would have bet money Daysy had no interest in or gift for domestic design.

If José Maria wasn't a liar he suffered from amnesia. He told Xavier he never had a daughter named Lourdes. A grinning idiot, Xavier heard him out, listened to the breakers breaking percussively behind them. The Zarzuela kids moved off to play soccer. Daysy, bony in a hungry way in her yellow shiftlike dress, sucked in her cheeks and squinted in imitation of her husband. There was salt in the wind. The entire proximate world was listening to catch out the fisherman in his lie. Had to be a mistake.

"My problem," Lourdes had told Xavier, "is I'm always wanting more than I can get."

They were standing in Freezer 2-B in a meat-packing plant in Buffalo. A vegetarian since he was twelve, Xavier had thought eight hours a day among all those sides and hindquarters and bloody hunks of beef might teach him something about need, and bodies, and therefore the composition of the world. Plus he needed a job. After a certain point it was no longer tenable to continue pretending to work on a dissertation. But he had only gone into graduate-school Spanish after he could no longer pretend he might return to the seminary.

He had an ear for the Spanish, which made it easy to get next to the olive woman from Honduras who showed up one day at Queen City Beef.

"You're too beautiful to be doing this for a living," he told her. If he had tried to construct an introduction he could not have done better than the line that popped out. She understood it was not a lounge-lizard come on, it was naked truth.

"A person has to eat," she told him, which justified for Xavier all the ugly months he had spent in the company of frozen cow parts.

Before they left 2-B she told him how she had made up her mind to leave Honduras. Restless in the village of her forefathers, she took a bus to Tegucigalpa, a green and rocky capital in the hills. All she took to invest was her looks, which were enough to get her an easy job as a receptionist in a bank. She lived small, saved her money against the crisis that was coming. It came. The bank manager was an exiled Nicaraguan with the temerity to call himself a refugee, which was the story he developed in order to pity himself with conviction.

He called Lourdes to his office. He told her he admired her, and he was lonely. His wife, a Cuban conservative, was having an affair with a junior political attaché at the American Embassy. There was no proof, but the wound went deep. He needed healing. He was standing close enough for Lourdes to smell his breath. She smelled Scotch, and onions, and, overpoweringly, beef. Involuntarily she inhaled. Steak vapors made her sick to her stomach. She told him she needed some time.

What she needed the time for was to convince the man with the hostile mustache behind bulletproof glass in the U.S. consulate that she was not intending to emigrate to Gringolandia. Strictly speaking she wasn't intending anything. The only thing on her mind was getting away from Honduras. What might happen at the other end of the airplane ride had no reality in her mind. That fuzziness probably helped convince the mustache. She received a one-entry visa. And entered. Even though it cost a lot more in the U.S., once there she ate only fish.

José Maria Zarzuela had been experiencing spasms of serious pain in his lower back, debilitating enough to keep him out of his boat. The lack of fish to sell had to be the real cause of Daysy's anxiety. Hypersensitive, at first Xavier thought she was rejecting him, but when he tried to leave she was the more forceful in insisting he stay. Visitors almost never showed up on their beach. A gringo looking for his lost Latin lover was a valuable distraction. So he stayed. He needed time to study their faces, to look for lies and/or a family resemblance.

It was midmorning, the sun not yet up to maximum strength. José Maria brought out a bottle of rum and squeezed the juice from some grapefruits. Daysy disappeared behind the house to boil something for lunch, and the two men shared a glass of equal parts of rum and grapefruit.

The rum revealed José Maria's secret: He was a religious man, in a vindictive and visionary way. Getting slowly sloshed, he told Xavier about the several times he had seen Mother Mary on the water. She appeared in the form of an actual woman of flesh and blood. She wore blue, and her brown hands were arthritic and work worn, with large, swollen knuckles. She told José Maria that the second time around Jesus would be born in the house of a fisherman. And that she herself couldn't help taking sides with the people who worked with their hands and their backs; she found the spiritual needs of the rich less interesting, more predictable, and frequently oily.

The fisherman was generous enough to stand Xavier with the workers of the world among whom Jesus was going to spend his second coming. He reserved his rancor for the faceless, unfeeling minority who ran the world and ate his fish at a distance off silver plates. By noon both of them were drunk. Daysy served them fish chowder, and sincere messages of love and fellow feeling went shuttling back and forth between the Zarzuelas and their visitor. When he left, the fisherman embraced Xavier with tears in his eyes and told him he wished he had a daughter named Lourdes because the name was beautiful and because then he wouldn't have disappointed the young *norteamericano*.

The walk back into San Cocho was hot, and slow, and rum colored. Then, a block before the dry-goods store, for the first time he caught sight of the doctor in the tropical suit. Going around a corner; gone. If he noticed Xavier he didn't let on. That was odd, in an isolated village in which being foreign would normally bond. But Xavier was relieved. Even at a distance the man was repulsive. He realized that his search for Lourdes had unbalanced him when he aimed a blind arrow of anger at the man just for being there, briefly visible.

The second sighting was even odder. The slack, gossipy woman who owned the dry-goods store told Xavier that a woman matching his description of Lourdes used to live in a village to the northeast. He did not discount the possibility that the woman was building up false hopes in order to keep her room rented a little longer, but he had come to Honduras to look for Lourdes. He looked.

Buses went infrequently to San Cristóbal de los Barcos Hundidos, so he walked. It took the better part of a long morning. On the outskirts of the village a cavernous 1950-something Dodge, black and mysteriously beautiful, passed him going north. Before the dust stirred and blocked his view Xavier recognized the passenger in the backseat behind the driver, who looked like a fisherman of some kind, ill at ease behind the wheel. The doctor didn't even look out the window at the sunburnt gringo with sore feet. Going; gone.

In San Cristóbal de los Barcos Hundidos there was no one like Lourdes.

In his room, Xavier waited until he was absolutely sure the man had tiptoed back down the precarious steps. He was thinking about sitting up for a long time. Then he sat up. His landlady had given him some horse pills she swore would defeat the dengue. He believed her. But the medicine hadn't kicked in yet, and moving his body involved a conscious act of will that took time.

He sat, finally, in the sparkling space the hallucinatory bird had occupied, and thought about God. Specifically, their relationship. It was characterized by endless longing, the way romantics parsed absence and embraced the conundrum.

He had the sense that he had blundered his way close to a truth that mattered. It had to do with God's own need, its wellspring in love and longing, and the burden of loving back it placed on merely human shoulders. He was thankful for living in a century in which ascribing questionable qualities to God wasn't going to get him roasted on a spit of orthodox outrage.

He could put up with the dengue. He could put up with the hallucinations. What he couldn't tolerate was the drag his illness put on looking for Lourdes. He did not wish to be alone any longer than he had to be.

He was thirty-three, old enough to distinguish the varieties of aloneness typical of his time. He had seen people burn out in divorce and enter a state of perpetual reflective hibernation, narcissism revisited with pain attendant. Others he had observed succumb to routine or to expectations (met and unmet) and then sanctify their disappointments by constantly reenacting them. He had witnessed the deadly stasis people entered in the presence of television, or a computer, or the Buffalo Bills. He wanted none of that. What he wanted was Lourdes.

They were together a month in Buffalo, all the time she lasted at Queen City Beef. In retrospect, the clarity and ease with which they came together may have had something to do with their separate senses of how short it was going to be. The day after they met in the freezer, they made love. The day after they made love, she moved into his apartment in Black Rock. The day after she moved in, they told each other their secret stories. The day after they learned each other's stories, they began guiding themselves toward a future neither one alone could quite envision.

"You're a God-struck man," she told him. "You're a seeker. But you're not meant to be a monk. Being a priest would have killed you. It was a self-defense instinct that held you back. That was healthy. What you need now is to figure out how you will go on seeking."

Living with Lourdes did wonders for Xavier's Spanish. It

bloomed. "You're looking, too," he told her. "Not for God, though. You're looking for perfect love, from an imperfect man. What you want is love that doesn't calculate, that doesn't figure your beauty in some kind of compatibility equation and want something back."

He thought he was articulating what he was going to give her, but he was too smart by half. The note she left after the month was a gracious thank-you and an acknowledgment that he was right about what she wanted. She hadn't known it herself until he told her, and now she was going to go get it.

For a while he thought that mourning her loss was going to turn his hair prematurely gray, the shock was that profound. But his hair stayed black, and he survived. They wanted to make him a foreman at Queen City Beef. He was reliable, he could plan ahead, he cursed infrequently. He was, in fact, seriously overqualified. The day after they made him an offer he quit. The remarkable fact was his year-and-a-half drift before heading south to pick up Lourdes's trail at the source, in Honduras, her home. If it wasn't for the dengue . . .

★ ★ ★

Finally. He was coming out of a tube, or else a tunnel. Something round and sloping, anyway, with a treacherous floor. It was like opening your eyes after a lifetime of hibernation to find yourself inside the one fantasy you really needed to come true. He saw her from a long way off, started running across the sand toward her. She was dancing. That had been one of his chief regrets, that they hadn't danced together in Buffalo. There had been no time. The evening wind off the Caribbean wasn't cool but it refreshed as it brushed. There was enough to tangle her hair, which was enough to make him salivate and remember sex. When he got close he saw the sweat beaded on her face. He stopped. Barefoot, her heels digging short-lived holes in the wet sand, she stopped dancing long enough to register surprise. Or was it pleasure? He smelled lemon, wondered whether it was something on her amazing pneumatic body or in the air. Didn't matter.

"It's a game," she told him. She was smiling, self-satisfied. Her attention was only partly on him, which irked. "I didn't know you knew how to play it."

"I learned." It wasn't wise to let his disappointment show.

She nodded, dancing again, and he was pleased to be able to please her with the correct answer. Then he was also dancing, alongside her in a way that was with her, part of what she was doing, and also separate. There had been a small fire inside a ring of smoke-blackened stones. They went around the ring in a rhythm that required no music, because they were the music or else it was inside them. He was barefoot, too. The scratch of cool sand on the soles of his feet was stimulating, even erotic.

When they stopped to breathe he tried to tell her about looking for her, but she shook her head. "It's not about looking," she corrected him.

"Then what?" He didn't like admitting his ignorance. He thought it might eliminate him from serious contention, draw him away from her magic circle and the dance, but the fear of missing out on something he should know temporarily overruled his caution.

"Being here," she explained the way a careless parent would toss off something in a hurry to a child who was slow. The irritation was not completely masked. "That's all. Look." She pointed to a single-masted sailboat, tiny in the distance on the water, elegant and graceful in the way it skimmed. He felt an overpowering desire to ride the boat with her.

"I know," she told him, though he had said nothing.

Dancing. The sailboat moved steadily but slowly in their direction. Eventually, rounding the ring, he made out a design on the flapping white sail: a stylized gull, maybe, with outstretched wings. Not once, not ever, had he felt this kind of exultation, this heady combination of peace and pleasure and expectation.

So that the black Dodge's showing up above them on the beach, on the sharp green line cut by the sea oats, took him by surprise. She stopped dancing as soon as she saw it, shrugged her shoulders. She was miffed, he could see that, but not as upset as she should have been.

"They're waiting for you."

"No," he told her. "I won't go."

"Suit yourself."

What convinced him to pick up his feet and walk toward the parked Dodge was what he perceived as her indifference. It bruised. Whatever had happened was over. He would not look back to see whether she was dancing again, alone around the fire stones. He concentrated on his feet, which were kicking up little jets of sand.

The driver was the same misplaced fisherman who had been driving the car in San Cristóbal de los Barcos Hundidos. As soon as Xavier slid into the backseat next to the doctor, the driver eased the old car into low gear, backed it off the beach onto the highway. Everything was the way it had to be. Xavier saw that, although understanding didn't mean accepting, let alone liking it.

The same white suit, wrinkled but clean. Out of an inside breast pocket the doctor drew a handkerchief and offered it to Xavier, who refused. There was a medicinal smell about the man, sore-muscle liniment mixed with camphor, and a satisfying old-leather smell that could have come from the seats of the Dodge, which was in terrific condition. When he spoke, Xavier was surprised by the delicate timbre of his voice. He spoke native English but with an accent Xavier could not connect with a specific place. Hearing the voice changed for the better the opinion he had formed about the man.

"It's not me," he told Xavier, though that was obvious now. "I'm just the errand boy, as it were." He whistled a folklike melody through his teeth.

"Tell me where you're taking me." The question was formulaic; it was expected of him. It was important to go through these motions.

"A piece of advice." The doctor tapped the window glass beside him with a thumbnail, nodded at a high-shouldered brown hawk bobbing on a tree branch. He was evidently enjoying his assignment.

"I don't want advice."

He continued as though Xavier had not spoken. "When the time comes, don't posture. The predictable responses, the traditional excuses, an eloquent protestation of innocence and good intentions—none of that will get you where you want to go. A well-meaning meditation on guilt, for example, will absolutely fall flat. I speak, I might add, from experience. Don't suppose you are the first to find yourself in this . . . situation."

"Situation?"

"In this car. Let's leave it at that. The shorthand serves a purpose."

"What purpose?"

There was a logic here worth understanding. Xavier had to discipline himself not to push. He didn't want to seem overeager. Surprisingly, he felt braced rather than exhausted, not exactly calm but capable of withstanding the debilitating effects of anxiety. He was not about to corrode into nothingness.

Already they seemed to have been traveling miles. Without his noticing they had left the sea and the beach behind. The landscape through which they passed was desertlike, if not an actual desert. On both sides of the road ran ranges of low, wind-abraded dunes. The sand was khaki-colored. He wished it were white, then retracted the wish as simplistic and wrongheaded. Too bad he was no good at guessing directions; it was impossible to know which way they were heading. The sun was no help. It was lost behind a gray film that coated the sky thickly enough that no telltale luminescence was visible in any corner of the heavens. He reminded himself that it didn't matter. They rode with the windows open. The hot wind lashed.

Xavier was not inclined to chat with his escort, who needed no entertaining. He dozed fitfully, going in and out of a state that was like floating on a raft on the surface of a body of water on which the waves rolled and lifted, rolled and lifted ponderously. Once, the doctor woke him by touching his forearm lightly to point out a formation of long-winged, long-beaked, mustard-colored birds winging low and purposeful across the infinitely stretched gray sky. Melancholy, Xavier told himself, that's what their instinct tells them to escape. The unexpected insight was cause for some small satisfaction. But the deep, starred dark and the high-walled courtyard and the odor of night-blooming jasmine and fresh coffee took him by surprise, as though the miles from Lourdes at the beach to the cell into which they showed him had all been sleight of hand.

No light in the cell, but Xavier didn't want one. He listened to the doctor's heels clacking quietly going away, then coming back again. He took the cup of coffee the man handed him. It was sweet, strong, foreign.

"You're one of the quick ones," the doctor observed him through the bars. "I watched you while you slept, in the car. But the way things work around here, I'm obliged to point out the obvious regardless: This is not incarceration. Not in the usual sense."

"I know that."

The doctor nodded, cocked his head so that his jowls quivered, shrugged. "So be it, then. My duty is discharged. You're on your own."

Which didn't protect Xavier from a knee-weakening sensation of abandonment when the big fat man in the white suit disappeared into the darkness, heels complaining on the tiles, the sound sending back little echoes that confused the ear. He knew the doctor was gone for good. Not that he owed the man anything. His officiousness grated.

Having slept, Xavier couldn't just lie down on the cot, which had a tolerable mattress, and close his eyes. He sat instead in the ladderback wooden chair that was the cell's only other furnishing and finished in measured sips the sweet, strange coffee. There were important differences between looking and waiting, he reminded himself, but his brain was working slowly, he couldn't put into words the sense of those differences, which for current practical purposes made them moot.

He must have slept, though, because here came false dawn, and domestic animals stirring in the compound and the courtyard beyond. A rooster sneezed in its sleep, and a cat padding past Xavier's cell looked at him with indifferent eyes that brought back Lourdes's indifference on the beach the day before. That was the problem with being overly sensitive; it threw off your judgment.

Part of the ritual, if that was the word, involved leaving him alone for a while. The fisherman-chauffeur showed up with breakfast—a hard roll and a scoop of marmalade, a small glass of grapefruit juice, and a jug of the same pungent, unusual coffee. He enjoyed the meal, though there was something supercilious about the fisherman that irritated him.

Two mistakes were to be avoided. Fixating on the particulars of the place he was being held was a natural reaction. It was healthy curiosity that led him to pay such close attention to what he could pick up from his new surroundings: the practical sounds of laborers, men and women, going about morning tasks they had been doing for so long there was no resistance left in their bodies, and they took pleasure in doing what they knew. The metallic chatter of a diesel engine warming up in the courtyard. A donkey honking, and the lulling sensation of being in a wholly self-contained, self-referential little community. All of it, seen and unseen, exerted the pull of the mysterious on him. Novelty charmed. But real and necessary as it might be, it was only scenery. Where was not What, or it was only a part of it.

The opposite mistake would be to fixate on himself: his feelings, his moment-by-moment reactions, the fluttering minutiae of his keyed-up consciousness. To avoid that he did some calisthenics, ignoring the thin skin of grainy dirt covering the tile floor. Then, since there was nothing to read, he paced the cell doing a different sort of exercise. He selected a memory—the firs around the lake on his first day in the seminary, the time he got lost on the walk home from kindergarten and a king-size dog with penetrating yellow eyes showed up to protect him from bullies and guide him home, the first time he smoked marijuana with a naked woman and dope smoke made an aromatic cloud around her curly head—and he worked to bring back the details of the moment. He had read that with time and attention you could recreate an immense amount of your life. And it worked, so that instead of being tedious his first day in confinement was liberating, like being born again only better because of the pleasures of hindsight.

Nevertheless he was famished when evening came and then the desert night, so quickly cool. He was relieved to hear the fisherman-driver bringing a plate of food in his direction. Except that it wasn't the fisherman, it was an old man, caped and cowled, his face invisible in shadow, his body shapeless in a black robe. Xavier accepted the meal he was offered: a sausage and a hunk of white cheese, a piece of crusty bread and a glass of red wine, a mottled yellow pear. He did not try too hard to get a look at the hidden face; he would not leave himself open to a charge of bad manners.

"First, eat," the man told him, sitting on a three-legged wooden stool Xavier had not noticed in the corridor.

He ate. The man's voice was extraordinary: sweet and rich, the deep brown sediment in a cup of cocoa. The voice was a sign—the prow—of the man's commanding, compelling presence, which worked on Xavier with the force of a strong narcotic except that his mind was clear, clearer than ever. I don't care how this turns out, he told himself, it's worth it.

"You're comfortable?" the man asked after he had finished eating, saving the pear for later.

"Completely."

The cowl moved a little, the body shifted on the stool. "Tell me what you think is at the heart of all this, please."

"Love and desire," Xavier told him promptly.

"Be specific."

"Being pulled in opposite directions. Incessantly and without hope of resolution."

"Then your idea is to set up a clever dichotomy and hope I'll knock it into kingdom come with a single blinding insight."

"I don't have any expectations."

But that only angered the man. "Don't waste my time with stratagems." He stood up, held a hand out for the empty plate, left unceremoniously down the hall, the folds of his robe swishing dryly. Xavier knew better than to call him back.

The interview, for lack of a better word, had drained him. He lay on the cot and closed his eyes, slept as though he'd been digging ditches all day.

Sometime in the middle of the night an anxiety attack woke him. What if the man's anger had not been part of the ritual? What if Xavier's facile comeback had alienated him for good? Anything was possible, including being left where he was indefinitely because he wasn't sufficiently prepared, or interesting, or straightforward. Dread seeped into the cell like a noxious gas against which he couldn't possibly hold his breath long enough. He understood his mistake: He had wanted to be in control, to predict every step and stage of the experience, to identify the ritual, to handle what was happening to him the moment it happened. It was a form of hubris. But it was gone, and the space it left around him filled up with dread, which had its own color. He was a fool.

The night was interminable, but not as long as the next day. A ragged servant in blue with a patch on one eye and a gimpy leg brought him his meals, delivering the food as if to an animal that could not be expected to respond, and Xavier waited, fretted, girded himself up against the waves of anxiety that swept over and pounded him. By the evening he was a wreck, vulnerable and jumpy, which was how he assumed they wanted him to be. But they let him ride out another night alone, another intolerable day in which the hot desert air hung on him like a straitjacket and the erratic laughter of the workers in the compound lacerated. He knew they were laughing at him.

When the man in the black robe finally returned, on the evening of the second day he was left alone, Xavier was ready to trade whatever he had left of an honorable sense of self for some assurance. "I'm sorry," he told the man, who waved an arm to shut him up.

"Let me tell you the two most intelligent things you've done so far," he said.

The extraordinary voice was like a stun gun; Xavier slumped. "Okay."

"The first was entering the seminary. And the second was leaving it."

"I guess I knew that."

"And you've had luck. More than many. More than most, in fact."

"You mean running into Lourdes."

"I mean being born hungry."

"And then staying that way . . ."

The black cowl nodded, and for the first time since he got into the Dodge Xavier felt a tremor of hope. So he had tried too hard to control, to understand, to see everything as part of a ritual. A single mistake no matter how egregious need not condemn him for good. He was eager for the conversation to last, and it did. The black night of the courtyard was velvet, cool, comforting. The jasmine bled its sweet smell steadily into the absorbent air. A man laughed, then a woman, and a dog barked a long way off. And the interview—Xavier could come up with no better word—went on at a pace of its own, which made him feel remarkably secure.

That security, ironically, turned out to be the problem. After his night of long anxiety he had been ready to surrender any independence he had for something that would anchor him. And surrender he did. There followed pleasantly long nights in the company of the black-robed keeper that gave him what he required: focused conversation, a challenge to his habitual ways of thinking, care for the things that mattered. And, above all, the curious certainty that no matter how he responded the man in the black robe had seen it coming and was ready to point him to what needed to happen next.

So that when he mentioned almost casually to Xavier that they would be releasing him the next morning, he was free to go, Xavier panicked.

"I'm not ready."

"Your state of readiness doesn't interest me. In fact I find your obsession with the subject of yourself unimaginative. It's one reason you've failed to discover the obvious."

"The obvious what?"

"The obvious fact that this whole experience is about being free. You want a blessing on your adventure. But things don't work that way, if they ever did. I for one don't believe they did."

"No. I won't leave. This is where I belong. I've been trying for too long to get here."

The cowl shook, presumably with laughter.

"At least tell me whether I'm going about it the right way," Xavier pleaded. Groveling no longer bothered him the way it might have once. "I deserve that much. I've earned it." The self-pity tasted like copper in the bottom of his throat.

More laughter, of the gentlest, most infuriating sort. "Sorry. Evidently you still don't understand the process. The best I can do is clarify for you what it is you're doing. The scope of the project, to borrow a phrase from the bureaucrats."

"Then tell me."

"You're sure you want to know, Xavier . . ." It was the first time the keeper had used his name, which jolting intimacy forced Xavier to recognize that his stay in the compound was indisputably over.

"I'm sure."

The answer hit like new knowledge. It was the last thing he expected to hear. The shock had to do with recognition. "It's simple," the man told him quietly in his rich cocoa voice. "You're looking for Lourdes."

The keeper rose from the stool on which he invariably sat for the duration of the interview. With one enormously strong hand that felt like a claw he grasped Xavier's forearm and squeezed hard, and then he was gone, laughing down the dark hall.

Xavier's last night on the compound was as anxiety-ridden, as diffused with dread, as the first bad night had been. In the morning, haggard and oversensitive, he took the fat doctor's joke poorly.

"Cigarette?" the man in the same rumpled tropical suit asked with phony servility as he unlocked the cell door and beckoned for Xavier to step out. "Blindfold? One last cheeseburger?"

"I'm leaving," Xavier told him stubbornly. And he was. Out of the cell, through the courtyard, where workers in dark blue uniforms stared at him incuriously, into the waiting Dodge. The doctor heaved his great bulk in beside him on the bench seat, sighing dramatically. That he could take, all of it. What he couldn't abide was the slurred expression of complicity on the face of the fisherman-driver as he adjusted his rearview mirror and then knocked the gearshift lever on the column carelessly into first. I'm going, Xavier reminded himself, and he was gone.

★   ★   ★

The great thing about having a body was getting back to it. The longer the absence the sweeter the savor of homecoming. He opened his eyes and stared around him, listened to the blood pump through his heart, his veins, his arteries. One foot was asleep. He wiggled his toes until the feeling came back into them, enjoying the starburst sensation there. He supposed he had an erection. He allowed it to subside.

He had never really taken the time to appreciate the patterns of randomness in the paint peeling on the dry-goods woman's walls, or the pleasure produced for the eye by the particular shade of bottle green she had chosen. He took the time now. And the time to study the pale blue enamel pitcher, the matching basin on the bureau, the marble top of which was interestingly cracked. He observed the thin white towels hanging from nails in the wooden shutters. Yes indeed. Where, he had to admit, was among the more luminous parts of What.

Knocking. He didn't fight it, didn't cringe or avoid. It did take time to get from the bed to the door, but there like an earthly vision was his landlady in a blue housedress with flowers the size and shape of brussels sprouts. In her Caribbean Spanish voice was mixed the dust that had accumulated on every unsold item on her shelves below, and gossip, and sea salt, and something that smelled like essence of coconut. When she smiled he decided it would be easier to count the teeth than the empty spaces in her mouth.

"¿Está bién, Señor Javier?" she wanted to know.

He was fine. Fine.

"She was here. The one you're looking for."

"When?"

"You've been sick. You better now?"

"Where is she?"

The woman shrugged. She was not trying to be malicious.

"What about the car?" he asked her. The strong feeling that made him take her by the arm and shake it was not anger, nothing like that. *Giddy* was a better word for what he was. He was high, high and climbing.

"Not here."

"That's okay," he told her.

He squeezed past her on the narrow landing, took the stairs down slowly, one at a time, because his body wobbled. Some of the steps creaked under his weight. He had been sick, he reminded himself. At the bottom, on solid ground again, he remembered his landlady. He turned back, shaded his eyes against the glare, and looked back at her on the landing above. He didn't think he owed her any money.

"Good-bye," he called to her. His voice seemed to have an echo, but that may have been just his swollen perception, a hangover from the dengue.

He had an idea of where the Dodge was parked, or might be. Just a hunch, but that was enough, for the moment. He had momentum, the purpose of which was carrying.

"Señor Javier," the landlady called down through cupped brown hands. "Where are you going? What are you doing?"

He realized she meant him. But he had his answer ready, white rabbit out of black top hat.

"I'm looking for Lourdes," he told her. Because he was. He went.